# ELEANOR ROOSEVELT'S IN MY GARAGE!

## Also Available in the History Pals Series

*Ben Franklin's in My Bathroom!*

## Other Books by Candace Fleming

FICTION

*The Fabled Fourth Graders of Aesop Elementary School*

*The Fabled Fifth Graders of Aesop Elementary School*

NONFICTION

*Amelia Lost: The Life and Disappearance of Amelia Earhart*

*The Great and Only Barnum: The Tremendous, Stupendous Life of Showman P. T. Barnum*

*The Lincolns*

*On the Day I Died*

# ELEANOR ROOSEVELT'S IN MY GARAGE!

### HISTORY PALS #2

## CANDACE FLEMING

#### WITH ILLUSTRATIONS BY MARK FEARING

schwartz & wade books • new york

Text copyright © 2018 by Hungry Bunny, Inc.
Jacket art and interior illustrations copyright © 2018 by Mark Fearing

All rights reserved. Published in the United States by Schwartz & Wade Books, an imprint of Random House Children's Books, a division of Penguin Random House LLC, New York.

Schwartz & Wade Books and the colophon are trademarks of Penguin Random House LLC.

Visit us on the Web! rhcbooks.com

Educators and librarians, for a variety of teaching tools, visit us at RHTeachersLibrarians.com

Library of Congress Cataloging-in-Publication Data is available upon request.
ISBN 978-1-5247-6786-0 (hc) — ISBN 978-1-5247-6787-7 (lib. bdg.)
ISBN 978-1-5247-6788-4 (ebook)

The text of this book is set in 14-point font Adobe Caslon.
The illustrations were rendered in pencil and digitally manipulated.
Book design by Rachael Cole

Printed in the United States of America
2 4 6 8 10 9 7 5 3 1
First Edition

To Annie . . . who is definitely blabworthy!
—C.F.

For Lily Emma. You can change the world.
—M.F.

# CHAPTER ONE

I groaned at the picture. Why, oh why, had Mom sent my little sister to technology day camp? Seriously. Second graders should *not* be allowed to text. It's just annoying. I tapped out a reply to tell her to stop.

Believe it or not, she did.

My phone went quiet.

Too bad it was the only thing that got quiet. "FD?" shouted the woman in my closet. She pounded on the door. "This is out-rageous. I insist you let me out this instant!"

Just so you know, I am not FD. And I was pretty sure I'd never met FD. In fact,

I was pretty sure I'd never met the woman in my closet, either, except in the pages of some boring social studies book, or in a musty history museum, or maybe during one of my teacher Mr. Druff's long, snore-fest lectures about "the incredible story that is America's past." He actually said that. He made us write it down in our social studies notebooks too.

"FD, are you still pouting about your speech to Congress?" the woman called out. "Truly, darling, no one noticed your zipper was down."

I knew I had to open the door. I also knew that the second I did, things were going to get way out of control. I am not exaggerating. I'd experienced this blast from the past once before, and I needed just a few more minutes to brace myself. I mean, it wasn't like I'd been expecting any . . . um . . . visitors today.

An hour earlier, my day had been pretty

normal. I'd been lying on the family-room sofa reading another graphic novel—this one about an alien kid who crashed on Earth—while my irritating little sister, Olive, danced around the house in her brand-new mermaid Princess Aquamarina bathing suit. She was singing at the top of her lungs too. "Party, party, par-TAY! party, party, par-TAY!"

At first, I'd tried to ignore her by burying my nose deeper in my book. I do both these things a lot—ignore my sister and read graphic novels.

I *love* graphic novels.

I do *not* love Olive when she's being annoying.

And boy, was she annoying. I knew she was really excited about the swimming party Mom was throwing for her eighth birthday that day. But geez, did she have to be such a pest?

"Knock it off," I'd growled.

Olive scrunched her face at me. "Party party poop-ER! Party party poop-ER!"

I slammed my book shut and stomped up to my room.

Of course, she followed. "Come on, Nolan. We're going to be late to my party."

"I'm ready, already," I grumbled.

Just as I was putting on my shoes . . .

*POP!* A bright light shot out from under

my closet door. It grew white . . . whiter . . . crystal white. From deep within came the sounds of static and faint voices. A second later, my bedroom filled with the sound of a gazillion bubbles popping all at once. Then . . .

*Bam! Bam! Bam!*

Someone started banging on the inside of my closet door.

"It's Ben!" Olive had cried. "He's come back for my birthday!"

She flung open the door.

Screamed.

And slammed it shut again.

"That," she panted, "is definitely *not* Ben Franklin."

"Hullooo!" came a woman's quavering voice. "FD? Is that you? Let me out, won't you? I seem to have gotten trapped."

At that moment, Mom hollered from downstairs. "Nolan! Olive! Is somebody up there with you?"

I swear our mother has the sharpest hearing in the universe. Maybe that's why she's the author-illustrator of the Bumble Bunny series of children's books. Big ears come naturally to her.

Mom didn't wait for us to reply. "It's getting late!" she shouted. "Time to go to the party!"

Olive yelped and looked from the bedroom door to the closet door. "Now what?"

"You go," I said urgently. "I'll stay with . . . with . . . whoever."

"But I'm dying to know who's in there," she whined. "I didn't recognize her." She reached for the knob. "Let's take another peek."

I leaped in front of her and pressed my back against the closet door. "And turn her loose in the house with Mom here? Are you crazy?"

"But—"

"You promised," I whispered through gritted teeth. "You promised to keep all this—the crystal radio, Ben Franklin time traveling here from history—a secret until we figured it out, remember?"

She made a pouty face.

"I know you're there, FD. I can hear you breathing," the woman in the closet called.

"Remember, Olive?"

She nodded slowly.

"Then go!" I said. "Try to act normal. And whatever you do, don't say a word about, er, *this*."

"Olive!" Mom called from the staircase.

"Coming, Mother dearest!" she shouted back in this ridiculous British accent she'd learned from watching PBS. She crossed the room and stepped out into the hallway. "Pish posh, but it's a lovely day for a party."

Believe it or not, *that* was normal for Olive.

"Nolan, are you coming?" Mom called up.

I came out of my bedroom and stood on the upstairs landing, peering down at her. "I . . . I can't."

"But it's your sister's birthday."

"It's *mermaid* swimming, Mom. With a bunch of giggling eight-year-old girls." I slapped on my most pathetic puppy-dog expression. "Please, can't you give a guy a break?"

"Do let him stay, Mummy," chimed in still-British Olive. "The big oaf will do nothing but ruin the party."

Mom looked at me with laser eyes for a second. Then she nodded. "But stay in the house. And no friends."

"No friends," I promised. I figured it wasn't a lie. How could the person in my closet be a friend if I'd never met her?

Mom looked at me another moment. Then they were gone.

And I was alone with the lady in the closet.

She knocked again. "Enough, FD. You've had your silly joke. Now open this door at once. Franklin? Did you hear me? I'm beginning to grow faint."

*So am I,* I thought.

My belly felt tight and fluttery, like it was filling with bats. Beating their wings. Crowding my chest. Squeezing the air from my lungs.

Hand shaking, I reached for the doorknob . . .

# CHAPTER TWO

**. . . AND STOPPED. WHAT IF** the person on the other side of the door was some kind of murderer? I mean, not everyone in history was nice. What about Al Capone, or Attila the Hun, or that lady who chopped people up with an ax?

The bats were really going crazy now.

I sat back down on my bed.

I sat there awhile.

*Buh-dop*, went my phone. I glanced at it.

*Buh-dop!*

*Buh-dop!*

Trust my sister to send selfies while I was fighting for my life.

Dropping the phone onto my bed, I snatched my baseball bat from its place in the corner and approached the door again.

"On three," I told myself. "One . . . two . . . THREE!"

I flung open the door.

And the woman stumbled out.

She wasn't an ax-wielding maniac or an old-time gangster.

She was a grandma.

She was tall, with sloped shoulders, and her white-gloved hands flapped at the ends of her arms like her wrists were hinged. Her front teeth stuck out, but her chin curved in. She had on a navy blue skirt, a white blouse, plain white tennis shoes, and . . . was that a *hairnet*? It was! A hairnet, just like the school lunch lady's. It covered her short, graying hair.

I searched my brain. She looked familiar, but . . . who was she?

With one white-gloved hand, she held her nose. With the other, she brushed a gym sock off her shoulder.

Oh, geez. Whoever she was, she'd had to climb over my dirty clothes pile to get out. I blushed. Good thing it was just a sock.

"Gracious! Good heavens!" She waved her hands in front of her face, sucking in fresh air. "What a stench! I was beginning to think I would never be set free. Honestly, Franklin—" She stopped abruptly. She blinked. She looked around and her brow furrowed. "This is *not* the White House," she said.

"No," I said. "And I'm not FD *or* Franklin."

"They are one and the same," she replied. "And that you are not him is patently obvious."

Her voice was high-pitched and fluttery; it made me think of a flock of small birds flying up and out of a cage. I could actually see the birds in my mind, flapping and thrashing against the bedroom ceiling. That's what happens when you read as many graphic novels as I do. You start to visualize *everything*.

"Well," the woman went on, "do you know where I might find him?"

"Who?" I asked.

She looked annoyed. "Franklin, of course. My husband, *and* thirty-second president of the United States—Franklin Delano Roosevelt."

I snapped my fingers. "I know you! You're Eleanor! Eleanor Roosevelt! We studied you last year in school."

"In your current events class, no doubt," she said.

"History class," I corrected her.

I searched my mind for what I'd learned about her. Facts came out in a spurt: "You . . . you worked for civil rights, and equal rights. When you were First Lady, people nicknamed you . . . um . . . Eleanor Every-where because . . . Wait, don't tell me. Be-cause you traveled everywhere for your husband. He was in a wheelchair, right? So he needed you to be his legs and go where he couldn't. You went all kinds of places First Ladies never went, like Nebraska cornfields and Virginia coal mines."

"Yes, that is correct," Mrs. Roosevelt re-plied. "But where am I *now*?"

I hesitated. "Maybe you should sit down for this."

"For what?"

I blurted out the truth. "You're not in Washington, D.C., anymore. You're in my bedroom—I'm Nolan Stanberry—in Roll-ing Hills, Illinois. You . . . you time traveled to the twenty-first century."

I waited for her to faint.

She didn't. She didn't start screaming or running around either. She didn't even need to put her head between her knees like Mom did the time she backed the car into that lamppost at Dunkin' Donuts.

She just stood there, rocking back and forth on her heels. I could tell by the way her lips tightened and her blue eyes took on a beaming sort of gaze that she was concentrating really hard.

"Um . . . Mrs. Roosevelt?" I said cautiously. "Are you okay?"

She didn't seem to hear me. She just kept rocking and looking the place over.

"Are you feeling sick or something?"

Mrs. Roosevelt blinked again. Then she walked over to my desk and with one gloved index finger started touching stuff: the lid of my closed laptop, my reading light, all three of my soccer trophies—one for each year I'd played. She paused at my calendar. With the same finger, she underlined the year once . . . twice . . . three times. She shook her head and stared at nothing for a few seconds.

Then she headed toward my bookshelf. On the way she touched some of the stuff on my walls: my Darth Vader poster, my Chicago Cubs World Series Championship pennant.

At first I thought she was checking for dirt. I saw that one time on the Science Channel. A guy wearing a pair of white gloves stuck his fingers into all the places in your house that never get cleaned, like the inside of the bathtub drain and under the refrigerator. It was pretty disgusting. I didn't think Mrs. Roosevelt was swabbing for gunk, though. I was pretty sure she was trying to deal with everything that had happened. Still, it was kind of weird.

She moved along my shelf, touching the spine of each one of my books. When she came to *Captain Blood,* my favorite graphic novel, she took it off the shelf, opened the cover, and stared at the copyright date before touching it once . . . twice . . . three times.

"'There are more things in heaven and earth, Horatio, than are dreamt of in your philosophy,'" she muttered.

Oh, geez, she wasn't making any sense. Did she lose her mind on the way to the twenty-first century? And why was she calling me Horatio?

"Nolan," I corrected her. "My name is Nolan."

She didn't reply. Instead, she headed out the bedroom door and down the hallway. As she went, she touched each of the family pictures that lined the wall from one end to the other. Pictures of Mom and Olive and me.

We used to have pictures of us with our dad, too, but after the divorce and his move to London, Mom put them away in the attic. Not all at once, but little by little, like he just faded off the walls.

Mrs. Roosevelt kept going. Like a sleep-walker, she went down the stairs, her finger tracing a path down the banister. In the kitchen, she touched the toaster and the blender. Her lips moved, but no sound came out.

I was really starting to worry. "Mrs. Roosevelt?"

She turned and opened the door leading into the garage. More touching. More muttering. She picked up the hedge clippers. She poked at the recycling bin. She ran a finger along the tool bench, then reached out and rang the bell on Olive's bicycle.

*CHA-CHING!*

Mrs. Roosevelt started and sort of shook herself. That faraway look faded from her eyes. "Yes, well, that is that," she said at last. She gave one brisk nod.

"Can I get you something?" I asked. "A glass of water? An aspirin? Maybe some cheesy doodles?" Cheesy doodles always calm my mom. When's she upset, she needs carbs.

Mrs. Roosevelt shook her head. "No, thank you."

I stepped closer to her. "Are you feeling okay?"

"I do admit to some nerves," she said. "A person never imagines herself traveling through time, after all."

"I guess not," I agreed.

"Still, I learned long ago that you have to accept whatever comes, and the only important thing is that you meet it with courage and the best you have to give." She straightened her shoulders. "I am ready to hear everything . . . um . . ."

"Nolan," I reminded her. "Nolan Stanberry."

She peered at me a second, her blue eyes high-beaming. Then she climbed up and settled herself on the seat of our riding mower. "Tell me everything, Nolan Stanberry." She rested her chin in her hands. "And please, spare no detail."

# CHAPTER THREE

**I'M NOT SURE HOW** long she sat there, staring across the garage at me like that. It seemed like a few hours, but it was probably only a minute or two. The thing was, I just didn't know where to start. I mean, how do you explain something you don't understand?

I plunged in. "It's been two weeks since someone traveled here through time. That was the only time until this time, and that time was almost two hundred and fifty years after his time, which is an earlier time—colonial times—than you, which is like 1940, right?"

Mrs. Roosevelt's brow was scrunched up in concentration. It made the knot of hairnet in the middle of her forehead look like a big black spider. I could tell she wasn't following my explanation. Every time she frowned, it made the hairnet spider look like it was moving. And right now, that spider was spinning a web.

"Just forget it," I said. "Let me start again."

"I would be most appreciative," said Mrs. Roosevelt.

I paused, pulling together my thoughts. At last I said, "This has happened once before, two weeks ago. That's when a mysterious package turned up on our front doorstep."

Mrs. Roosevelt leaned forward. "Go on."

"Inside was an antique wood box. It had

a hinged lid, and its sides were engraved with the words 'Property of H.H.'"

"And who is H.H.?"

I shook my head. "Olive—she's my sister—and I don't know. But when we opened the box's lid, we found an old-timey crystal radio.

"Of course we played with it," I went on, "and when we did, this crazy thing happened. The room got all blurry. And the headphones filled with static and pieces of conversation. And then—*poof!*—guess who was standing in our kitchen? Ben Franklin!

"While he was here, we learned to mermaid swim, and made an electrostatic machine, and got arrested and stuff," I said. "But maybe now isn't the time to tell you about that."

Mrs. Roosevelt's eyes were high-beaming again. "Do I understand you correctly? Are you saying this crystal radio is a time machine?"

I nodded.

"And you have told no one of its existence?"

I thought about our nosy neighbor, Tommy Tuttle. That sneaky snoop had *almost* learned the truth. Luckily, our secret was still safe. And I wanted to keep it that way.

"I can't explain it," I told Mrs. Roosevelt. "I just know deep down in my gut that we shouldn't tell anyone. Not even our mom. We need to keep this a secret. At least for now."

Mrs. Roosevelt nodded her understanding. "And where is this radio currently? It seems to me we should take a look at it without delay."

And that's when the big garage door

rolled up and a car *beep-beep*ed, pulled in, and stopped.

Olive scrambled out of the backseat. "Hey, Nolan. What are you doing in the garage?" She pointed at Mrs. Roosevelt, still perched on the lawn mower. "And *who* is that?"

"Eleanor!" exclaimed our mother, sliding out from behind the steering wheel. "You're here! And right on time too."

# CHAPTER FOUR

**"YOU *KNOW* HER?" SAID** Olive.

"Well, we've never met in person," replied Mom.

"No kidding," I muttered.

"But Eleanor does comes highly recommended," Mom continued. "Her experience and qualifications are impeccable . . ."

Mrs. Roosevelt stood and smoothed her skirt. "How kind of you to say."

". . . and her achievements are impressive."

"I merely do what I have to do," said Mrs. Roosevelt.

Mom smiled and shook Mrs. Roosevelt's hand. "I don't have a single qualm about leaving the children with you."

"Wait . . . what?" exclaimed Olive.

I shook my head. "Wh-what's going on?"

Mom put her hands on her hips. "Honestly, do you two ever listen to me?" she said. "I'm off to New York City this afternoon to plan publicity for the new book series. I told you last week, remember?"

Her new book series still featured the Bumble Bunnies. But instead of modern-day adventures, the bunnies were blasting to the past. That was the title of the series: The Bumble Bunnies Blast to the Past. In each book, they go back in time and meet historical figures. Guess who inspired the first one?

Mom still doesn't know the truth—that she actually met the real Ben Franklin. So how did she know about Eleanor Roosevelt? It didn't make any sense.

"But who is she?" whined my sister. "Where'd she come from? What'd she do?"

Olive stomped her foot. "And why are we still in the garage?"

"Calm down," I said.

"She's wearing a hairnet," said Olive. "Is she a famous lunch lady?"

"Her name," I began, "is Eleanor, um—"

"Ivey," finished Mom.

Mrs. Roosevelt blinked.

"Huh? Who's that?" asked Olive.

I shook my head again. "Ivey? As in Mrs. Ivey from down the street?"

Mrs. Ivey is our regular babysitter. She's a little scatterbrained. Whenever she phones the house, she says, "Hello, Roland? This is Mrs. Ivey from down the street."

She thinks my name is Roland. I'm not even kidding. And she calls Olive "Olga."

"That's *Delores* Ivey," said Mom. "This is her sister-in-law, *Eleanor* Ivey."

"Who?" said Olive. "I've never heard

of Eleanor Ivey. What famous stuff did she do?"

Mom chose not to answer her. "I know you kids like having Delores stay with you, but she isn't available. The poor dear is having her bunions removed."

"Ewww!" Olive gagged. A second later, she asked, "What's a bunion?"

Mom still didn't answer her. "Lucky for us, she recommended Eleanor."

My mind was scrambling to sort things out. What was going on here?

"Eleanor . . . ," I repeated slowly. "Mrs. Ivey's sister-in-law."

Mom must have thought my confusion was worry, because she came over and hugged me. "I won't be gone long. Just twenty-four hours. I'll be back by supper-time tomorrow. In the meantime, Eleanor here will be your babysitter. And I expect you both to be on your best behavior."

Mrs. Roosevelt blinked again.

My mouth dropped open. Was this really happening? Things like this only happened in wacky kids' books!

Mom glanced at her phone. "Look at the time! My taxi will be here any minute."

As if on cue, there came a honk from the curb.

I nearly fell over, I was so relieved. Our secret was safe for now. Mom didn't know that the woman standing in front of her was Eleanor Roosevelt. She'd mistaken the First Lady for the babysitter!

I pushed my mother toward the open garage door. "All righty, then. We'll see you tomorrow, Mom. Have a good trip."

I needed her to leave—*now*—before Olive or Mrs. Roosevelt said something to spill the beans.

"But my suitcase," said Mom. "It's upstairs."

I swear, I practically broke the speed of light racing to her bedroom and back. Shoving the suitcase at her, I pushed her toward the driveway. "Time to go."

"Not until I kiss Olive good-bye," said Mom. She leaned down to plant one on my sister's cheek, but her eyes got stuck on Mrs. Roosevelt. "Are you sure we haven't met? You look so familiar." She snapped her fingers. "I know! Didn't we meet that time in kickboxing class?"

The cab honked again.

I rushed Mom straight toward the street. "Don't you worry about us," I said as she got into the cab's backseat. "We're going to be great. Totally great. I mean, Eleanor's here. What could go wrong?"

## CHAPTER FIVE

**OLIVE AND THE FIRST** Lady had gone inside while I was helping Mom. Once she was gone, I hurried up the driveway, pressed the button that lowered the big garage door, and burst into the kitchen.

Mrs. Roosevelt was sitting by herself at the kitchen table.

"Where's Olive?" I asked.

"She said she had to 'take care of business,'" replied Mrs. Roosevelt. "She looked quite determined and, it seemed to me, very pleased with herself."

Uh-oh! A smug Olive is a troublemaking Olive.

I moved into the family room just as Olive was finishing up a phone conversation. She was using her "Aren't I adorable?" voice.

"Yes," she was saying. "That's right, she just showed up. Yes, out of the clear blue . . . Yes . . . Thank you. My mother appreciates everything you've done for us."

"Who is that?" I asked suspiciously.

"Can you hold just a quick sec?" Olive

said sweetly into the phone. Then, slapping her hand over the receiver, she turned to face me. "It's Mrs. Ivey from down the street."

"Mrs. Ivey from down the street?"

"Is there an echo in here?" Olive said. "We can't have two Eleanors in the house, can we? So I'm calling and canceling the other one."

"You're canceling her?"

"There *is* an echo in here." Olive rolled her eyes. "I told her that our aunt turned up unexpectedly, and that Mom had to catch a plane and you were carrying her suitcase to the cab, so I was the only one left to call and tell her that *her* Eleanor didn't need to come."

"You lied?"

"Not about Mom or the cab or you help-ing her," replied Olive. "That's three truths and only one lie."

"You lied."

"ECHO ... ECHO ... echo," she said, loud to soft. "Anyway, it's just a teensy fib, a little baby lie. And it'll give us some time to—"

"—figure out how to send her home," I finished.

"You're wellll-come," she replied in a singsongy voice. She put the phone back to her ear. "Sorry about that, Mrs. Ivey. Like I was saying . . . You what? . . . Right now? . . . This very minute?"

"What's happening?" I hissed.

Mrs. Roosevelt came into the room. "Children, I believe it is high time we took a look at your crystal radio."

Olive huffed into the phone. "Fine!" She thrust it at Mrs. Roosevelt. "Mrs. Ivey says she needs to speak to the grown-up in charge. Can you believe that? I don't think she trusts me!"

Mrs. Roosevelt hesitated before taking it.

"Don't tell her your real name," I whispered frantically. "Do not say 'Roosevelt.'"

Mrs. Roosevelt nodded and spoke into the phone. "Yes, hullo? . . . Yes, I am here with the children. . . . Yes, I *did* arrive most unexpectedly. . . . Yes, it was *very* sudden. . . . Yes . . . Yes . . . Yes . . . Yes, good-bye." She hung up.

"*Yes!*" cheered Olive, pumping her fists in the air. She skipped out of the family room.

I sighed and rubbed my face.

Olive skipped back into the family room. She tapped me on the shoulder.

"What's her real name?" she whispered. "Eleanor who?"

"Roosevelt," I answered.

"Eleanor Roosevelt." Olive looked disappointed. "Was she famous?"

"Why else would her face be on the back of the five-dollar bill?" I replied.

"She's on the five-dollar bill?"

I shook my head. "Not yet, but she will be soon."

Olive perked up. "Hey, Ellie!" she hollered. "You're a superstar! A hotshot! A big-deal diva!"

"It is Mrs. Roosevelt," the First Lady corrected her. "You may call me Mrs. Roosevelt."

Olive made a pouty face.

Mrs. Roosevelt ignored it. "Now let us see that crystal radio."

## CHAPTER SIX

**I'D HIDDEN THE CRYSTAL** radio way in the back of my closet at the bottom of a box of building blocks. After Ben's visit, Olive and I had agreed never to play with it again. So how had Eleanor gotten here? Was it some kind of magic? Had the radio learned to turn itself on? Or maybe it was H.H.'s doing.

I pulled the string attached to the overhead bulb. Light flooded the closet.

No, it wasn't magic that had worked the radio. Or H.H. It was . . .

"Olive!" I bellowed.

I grabbed the radio and thundered back down the stairs.

She took cover under the kitchen table. "I didn't mean to, Nolan. Honest. I played with it. Just for a minute. But it didn't work. No lights. No static. Nothing. I thought it was broken."

"It sounds as if your machine had a delayed reaction," said Mrs. Roosevelt.

"That's it!" Olive cried. "It was a relayed . . . derailed . . . um . . . like she said."

I gritted my teeth. "It's *your* fault Mrs.

Roosevelt is here," I hissed. "You promised never, ever to touch it. So why'd you do it?"

Olive's bottom lip trembled. "I just wanted Ben to come to my birthday party. Nobody swims as good as Ben. And ... and ..." A tear slipped down her cheek. "I miss him. He's my friend."

Oh, brother!

Mrs. Roosevelt crouched down and looked at Olive. "I understand completely," she said. "You made a mistake. Who has not done that? But now, Olive, it is time to learn from that mistake. You must promise yourself never to repeat it. You must become a better person because of it."

Olive rolled her eyes at me. "She's kind of a Mrs. Preachy Pants, huh?"

"She's right," I said. "Learn from your mistake, Olive, and promise never to touch the radio again."

Olive poked out her tongue at me. "And you're Mr. Preachy Pants." She turned back to Mrs. Roosevelt. "I feel better, though. You're a good babysitter, Ellie."

"Mrs. Roosevelt," insisted Mrs. Roosevelt.

"You'd be the *bestest* babysitter if you'd let me call you Ellie," said Olive.

Mrs. Roosevelt shook her head firmly.

Olive shrugged. "You can't blame a girl for trying." She crawled out from under the table. Then the three of us stared at the crystal radio, sitting dark and silent on the kitchen counter.

"Now then, children, let us not waste another moment," said Mrs. Roosevelt, suddenly all business. "I have mountains of work waiting for me at the White House—letters to answer, a newspaper column to write, a reception to host. I would like to be sent back immediately. I assume that other Eleanor person will still be willing to babysit?"

Olive gulped and pushed me forward. "You tell her, Nolan."

I made a face at my sister. Why did I always have to break the bad news? I turned to Mrs. Roosevelt. "The radio has one little . . . er . . . glitch."

"Glitch?" said Mrs. Roosevelt.

I nodded. "It won't return you to your time until . . . um . . . it decides you're ready."

Mrs. Roosevelt's eyebrows shot up past her hairnet spider. "And just how does it do that?"

"You have to learn something from us," I said.

"And we have to learn something from you," added Olive.

"I am not entirely sure I understand," said Mrs. Roosevelt.

I tried again. "We learn from the past how to live in the present. *And* vice versa."

"And what lesson must each of us learn?" asked Mrs. Roosevelt.

I shook my head. "We don't know."

"But once we learn whatever it is we're supposed to learn . . . *whammy!*" said Olive. "The radio will turn on. All by itself!"

Mrs. Roosevelt blinked. "So . . . *you* cannot reverse the process," she said slowly. "*You* have no control over sending me back."

I nodded. "That's right."

"Sorry," mumbled Olive. She looked down at her feet.

Mrs. Roosevelt blinked and started rocking back and forth on her heels again. She opened her mouth and closed it. Opened and closed it.

Opened and . . . She shook her head firmly.

"Well, then we must allow the radio to take its best course," she said.

"That's it?" I cried. "You don't want to scream or something?"

Mrs. Roosevelt frowned. "What would be the point? In times of trouble, one must keep calm and carry on."

"Hey, I have a T-shirt that says that," said Olive.

"I have a friend named Winston Churchill who says that," said Mrs. Roosevelt.

"Hey, I have a friend whose bulldog is named Winston Churchill," said Olive.

"I once had a bulldog named Olive," said Mrs. Roosevelt.

Olive put her hands on her hips. "Hey, are you kidding me?"

"Me? Kid?" Mrs. Roosevelt's voice sounded firm, but I swear I saw the corners of her lips start to twitch up into a smile. She quickly covered her mouth with a gloved hand.

"You are! You're a kidder, Ellie!"

Mrs. Roosevelt lowered her hand. "Mrs. Roosevelt," she corrected. "And I am not often a kidder. I am, however, very curious. Would you mind demonstrating what you did that brought me here? I wish to see every step."

"Okey-dokey," agreed Olive. She reached for the radio.

Warning bells started ringing in my head. I put out my hand. "Maybe we shouldn't—" I began.

But Olive had already grabbed the miniature lever that controlled the cat-whisker wire. She brushed it against the glinting stone that sat in a tiny brass bowl just below it.

The stone started to glow bright. White. Crystal white.

*Khhhh!* Static filled the headphones.

"I think I did it. Something's happening!" cried Olive.

"The device does appear to be awakening," said Mrs. Roosevelt hopefully.

Olive turned the dial two clicks.

"No, Olive, stop!" I cried.

*Khhhh!*

She turned it another click.

*Khhhh!*

"Olive!"

She turned it a third click.

*Khhhh!*

Then there was a sound.

Faraway. Tinny. Punctuated by static:
*Yip-yip . . . khhhh . . . yap-yap . . . khhhh . . .
arr-woof-woof-woof-woof . . . khhhh . . .*

I suddenly had a bad feeling. "Turn it off.
Don't—"

Too late. The hard edges of the room
blurred and fell out of focus, dissolving into
nothingness. Only the three of us appeared
to remain solid.

"What is happening?" called Mrs. Roosevelt.

"Hold on, Ellie!" cried Olive.

She grabbed for the First Lady, who sputtered, "M-Mrs. Roosevelt!"

Just like last time, my stomach lurched, and I got that sick feeling that comes when you watch a 3-D movie without the glasses. Off-kilter. Out of whack. Then—*POP!*—my ears rang with the sound of a gazillion bubbles bursting all at once.

The room snapped back into focus.

The queasy feeling passed.

A dog barked.

## CHAPTER SEVEN

**IN THE MIDDLE OF** the family room stood a fuzzy ball of black fur with a head too big for its body and a rubber bone in its mouth.

"It's a Scottie dog!" screeched Olive, making this tiny, high-pitched squeal that usually only dolphins can make. "A time-traveling Scottie dog!"

"Fala, my boy!" said Mrs. Roosevelt. She patted her knees. "Come here, you little rascal."

The dog stared at her for a second. Then his tail started whizzing around so fast I thought it would twist off his body. He flipped the rubber bone and caught it before he raced toward her and—toenails clicking on the hardwood floor—catapulted into her arms.

"Goodness, I hope Franklin doesn't notice you're gone," she said, hugging the dog close. "The last time you went missing he called out the National Guard."

*"Arrr-woof!"* Fala replied.

Mrs. Roosevelt set him on the floor and Olive squealed again.

"He's so *cuuute*! Isn't he cute, Nolan?" She flopped down next to him and wrapped her skinny arms around his neck.

"Adorable," I said. And I wasn't being sarcastic.

"Just like me," said Olive.

Oh, brother!

She started kissing the Scottie. "*Mwah!* You're cute enough to be a movie dog, you know that, Fala baby? *Mwah! Mwah! Mwah!*"

"He *is* a movie dog," remarked Mrs. Roosevelt.

Olive squealed a third time.

I slapped my hands over my ringing ears.

"Like in Hollywood?" shrieked Olive. "Like with lights . . . camera . . . addition?"

"Action," I corrected her.

She scrunched her nose at me. "Whatever."

"It was a short film, what Hollywood calls a one-reeler," continued Mrs. Roosevelt, "about a dog's life in the White House. . . ."

And as she told us about it, the pictures formed in my mind's eye. All the details. Just like in one of my graphic novels.

Oh, dear. Obviously, that is not them.

That is Fala — America's First Dog!

His high jinks charm everyone.

Americans from Maine to California adore him.

So it is hardly surprising that Hollywood comes calling. After all, people need something cheerful to take their minds off their worries. What better choice than Fala?

You're going to be the next Rin Tin Tin, old man.

You're going to be a movie star.

ARR-WOOF!

Hollywood types descend on the White House like a swarm of locusts.

They bring everything they need to make a successful film, except . . .

Please, Fala, work with us!

Come on, doggie. Act!

That's right. Fala *will* work for bacon.

Indeed, many memorable moments are caught on film that day.

The film makes Fala a star.

The President's
Dog

More importantly, it brings joy to Americans.

"Is his movie still around?" asked Olive when Mrs. Roosevelt had finished her story. "Can we see it on YouTube?"

Mrs. Roosevelt blinked. "Who tube?"

Outside the window, a twig snapped.

Fala's ears pricked, and Olive and I looked at each other.

"You don't think . . . ," she began.

I put my finger to my lips. Then I tiptoed out the back door and around the side of the house.

He was crouched behind the patio chaise lounge, wearing a pair of supersonic ears and a fake mustache and beard. He looked like a cross between Mickey Mouse and Bigfoot.

"Tommy Tuttle," I hissed.

Tommy froze for a second. Then he reached up and checked that his disguise was still in place. Nonchalantly, as if hiding behind outdoor furniture were as normal as answering the door, he stood and said, "So what blew my cover?"

I rolled my eyes. "You're joking, right?"

"I never joke about spying," he replied. He smirked and tapped one of his sonic ears. "I hear you have some visitors. Sounds like a yappy dog and a fluttery old lady."

"Get lost, Tommy."

Ignoring me, he reached into his pocket and took out a pencil and a notepad labeled *Crime-Solving Journal.* "The lady's voice. It sounds familiar. I know I've heard it before. Is she from history too? Like your last little friend?" he pressed. "What'd you say her name was?"

"I didn't," I said through gritted teeth.

"You might as well spill it," said Tommy. "No secret is safe when I'm on the case."

The bats were back, and flapping harder than ever. I clenched my fists. "Get. Off. My. Patio!"

He grinned and leaned in so close I could see a speck of peanut butter from his lunch in his fake mustache. "I warned you, Stanberry. No matter what it takes, no matter how long it takes, I'm going to get to the bottom of your secret. That radio sitting on your counter . . . when I figure out what it does, it's going to make me the most famous detective in the country. Who knows? I might even get my own reality show. Imagine it: *Tommy Tuttle, Kid PI.*"

"More like *Tommy Tuttle, Kid PU,*" I snapped back.

"Sticks and stones," said Tommy. He sauntered past me to where he'd hidden his bike in the bushes. I hate to admit it, but it blended in pretty well, what with all the camo tape wrapped around its frame, and the leaves and tree branches tied to the handlebars. He wheeled it onto the driveway and straddled it. Then he turned back to me. "Count on it, Stanberry. I'm going to crack this case wide open."

That was when the back door slammed open.

A second later, a ball of black fur bolted across the lawn.

"Puppy, come back!" shouted Olive. She ran into the yard, followed by Mrs. Roosevelt.

"I knew it!" exclaimed Tommy. He pointed at the First Lady. "You're . . . you're . . ." He snapped his fingers. "Somebody. I know it. You're . . . you're . . . *Argggggh!*"

Fala charged at Tommy. Racing around him in frantic circles, the dog jumped and yapped, his sharp little teeth snapping.

Tommy's know-it-all expression vanished. His mouth formed a bearded O, and his eyebrows shot past the headband of his supersonic ears. He screamed again. Then he put his feet to the pedals. Bike tires spitting gravel, he shot down the sidewalk.

Fala chased him to the edge of the yard.

*"Arr-roo-roo-roo-woof!"* The little guy almost sounded fierce.

"I cannot imagine what has gotten into him," said Mrs. Roosevelt. "Fala is usually so good-natured. He has never bitten anyone, not even a Republican."

"That's Tommy Tuttle," said Olive, as if that explained it. Which, actually, it did.

With a final growl, Fala gave up his guard-dog act. He started trotting around the yard, sniffing and lifting his leg on the birdbath, and the swing set, and the box-woods. . . .

"Ooh, he really had to go," said Olive.

"What do you expect?" I said. "He's held it more than eighty years."

. . . and Mom's potted geraniums, and—

A rabbit burst out from under the hostas.

In a flash, Fala went after it, zigging and zagging around the yard.

"Fala, no!" said Mrs. Roosevelt firmly.

*"Arrr-woo-woo-woo-woof!"*

He almost had the rabbit's puffy tail between his teeth when it suddenly bolted across the street.

Fala bolted after it.

"FAAA-LAAA!" shouted Olive.

The Scottie disappeared between the neighbors' yards.

## CHAPTER EIGHT

**MRS. ROOSEVELT DIDN'T FREAK** out. She didn't jump up and down or wave her fists in the air or anything. She just said, "Well, I guess we shall have to go after him."

She led an all-out sprint. I followed her. Olive followed me. Like some crazy movie chase scene, we darted through our neighbors' backyards, pushing through hedges and leaping over lawn furniture.

A little kid wearing a fire hat squirted us with a garden hose when we ran through her yard.

Two houses down from her, a snarling Chihuahua named Bonita chased us over a fence and into a yard where three snotty first graders started pelting us with mulberries from their tree house.

"I'll be back to deal with you guys later!" hollered Olive.

The boys stopped throwing.

My sister has a reputation.

We raced through the Tappletons' yard.

"There!" cried Mrs. Roosevelt, pointing.

A couple of houses away, Fala was lifting his leg on Mr. Jolly's prizewinning roses.

And Mr. Jolly was *not* so jolly about it. Waving a pink garden shovel, he burst out of his garden shed. His biceps with their bleeding dragon tattoos bulged. "You're toast, terrier!" he shouted.

Mrs. Roosevelt sprinted toward them.

Thinking to head the dog off from the opposite direction, I veered off course and cut through the Sanchezes' backyard.

"Wait for me! Wait for me!" cried Olive, trying to keep up.

Racing full speed ahead, I ducked under a line of flapping laundry, leaped over a border of boxwoods and . . .

*Ooomph!*

Plowed into Mrs. Roosevelt.

The two of us went down hard, knocking the wind out of me.

Olive came rushing up. She leaped onto my chest and started pounding on my heart to save my life. "Don't worry, Nolan. I saw how to do this on TV."

"Quit!" I gasped, shoving her off and staggering to my feet. My knee was scraped, and my tailbone felt bruised from the hard landing. I looked over at her. Her hairnet was crooked, and the palms of her white gloves were grass-stained.

"Are you alright?" I asked.

"Perfectly," she replied, getting to her feet. Olive whistled. "You're pretty fast for a . . ."

"First Lady?" interrupted Mrs. Roosevelt. "The position *has* built up my stamina. All that dashing about from meetings to receptions to press conferences"—she straightened her hairnet—"it's practically like training for the Olympics."

"Too bad we weren't fast enough to catch Fala," I said, looking around.

The dog was gone.

Mr. Jolly was still there, though. He shook his shovel at us before stomping back into his shed.

"Did you see which way the little rascal went?" Mrs. Roosevelt asked.

"Not me," said Olive. "I was too busy saving Nolan's life."

I rolled my eyes. "I didn't see either," I said, turning to Mrs. Roosevelt. "Sorry." I touched her arm sympathetically. I figured she must be feeling awful, what with losing her dog in the future and all.

Olive grabbed the First Lady's hand.

"Don't cry, Ellie. We'll find him. Fala will be okay!"

"Mrs. Roosevelt," Mrs. Roosevelt corrected. "And I am certainly *not* crying. Nor will I."

"Why not?" asked Olive. "Aren't you worried about speeding cars and mean dog-catchers and gangs of tough, snarling street dogs and—"

I elbowed her. "You can stop now," I hissed.

"Fala knows how to take care of himself," said Mrs. Roosevelt. "At least twice a week he slips out under the White House gate and goes off on an adventure. Why, just last week he got all the way to the Lincoln Memorial before the secret service found him." She smiled. "He was begging for food from a school group in his irresistable way. Oh, but that dog can put people under his spell. That is why Franklin calls Fala's begging 'the Treatment.'"

"But Fala's a stranger here," I said.

She nodded. "Which provokes the obvious question: Where would a dog go? Determine that . . ."

Olive chimed in, ". . . and then go there."

Mrs. Roosevelt nodded. "Exactly."

Olive got down on all fours and waggled her back end. "Thinking like a dog, pant-pant. Thinking like a dog."

"What about the town park?" I suggested.

"Shoe store!" shrieked Olive. She leaped to her feet and took off running.

## CHAPTER NINE

**MRS. ROOSEVELT AND I** caught up with Olive four blocks later. She was standing outside Sammy's Shoe Emporium, nose pressed against the front window, staring at a pair of high-tops covered in green, purple, and sea-blue rhinestones.

"The Princess Aquamarina Shimmer and Sparkle sneakers," she said dreamily.

"I knew it," I said. "You aren't looking for Fala. You're shopping for shoes!"

"Am not," argued Olive.

"Yeah?" I asked. "So tell me, what do shoes have to do with dogs?"

"Um . . . well . . . uh . . . dogs like to chew shoes, that's what." She thought a second. "*And* they carry around their owners' slippers."

Mrs. Roosevelt nodded. "I see your logic, Olive."

*Oh, brother!*

Olive shot me a smug look before opening the door.

What a madhouse! School was starting in just two weeks, and all around us kids were trying on shoes . . . taking off shoes . . . opening boxes . . . sending tissue paper flying . . . yelling, "I want these!" and "I hate those!"

One kid was throwing a temper tantrum because her dad wouldn't buy her fuzzy bunny slippers for kindergarten.

Another kid, a boy from Olive's class named Alden Wurlitzer, was sliding around the store in those foot-measuring things like they were ice skates.

The whole time, impatient parents held up shoes and barked out sizes at the store's one and only sales guy.

He rushed around, balancing a wobbly tower of shoe boxes taller than his head. "I'll be right with you!" "Just another moment, please!" "You wanted to try the slips-ons, not the sneakers?"

Alden skated into him.

The sales guy's tower of boxes went flying. A jumble of sneakers, boots, and other shoes scattered across the floor.

"My shoes!" cried Olive. She swooped up the Shimmer and Sparkle sneakers. "And what do you know? They're just my size."

"Put them down and let's get going," I said.

There was no way Fala had come in here.

But Olive had other ideas. Plopping down, she pulled off her sandals and slipped on the sneakers. She hopped up and down. The soles blinked like disco balls. "Their beauty is blinding!" she squealed.

I squinted, seeing green, blue, and purple spots in front of my eyes. "Pleeeease, take those off," I begged, then added, "We have to go."

"And turn our backs on a man in need?" exclaimed Mrs. Roosevelt.

It was the first thing she'd said since we came in. She pointed to the sales guy, who was on his hands and knees desperately trying to put the shoes back in their boxes.

"We must offer him our aid," she added.

And that's exactly what she did. Striding across the store, she extended her gloved hand to the sales guy and said, "I am here to help."

He grabbed it the way a drowning man grabs a rescue line. "Thank you. Bless you. Of all the days for my associate to be sick . . ." He stumbled to his feet. "You've sold shoes before?"

"Never," replied Mrs. Roosevelt. "Although I once did a radio show sponsored by the Shelby Shoe Company. Between my commentary on the newsworthy events of the day, I discussed the merits of brushed leather and hand stitching."

The sales guy hesitated. "Uhhh—"

"Beep-beep!" blared Alden. He skated into the children's shoe display, with its clown doll and circus decals. The doll tumbled off the table, landing in the lap of a little girl sitting crisscrossed on the floor. It grinned up at her with its powder-white face, beady black eyes, and big red lips.

The girl screamed.

Who could blame her? I mean . . . *clowns.*

The sales guy squeezed his eyes shut for a second. Then he opened them again, reached into his pocket, and pulled out a chrome shoehorn. He handed it to the First Lady.

The way she looked at it, you'd have thought it was a magic wand or something.

And maybe it was, because suddenly she whirled into action.

"Boots?" she said.

The sales guy motioned toward a set of floor-to-ceiling shelves at the back of the store. Leaping onto its sliding ladder, Mrs. Roosevelt glided toward the end of the shelves of shoe boxes. She slid the ladder to the Converse section and grabbed two boxes, then rode one-handed to the sandal section.

"Kids, don't try that at home!" whooped Olive. She did a little tap dance to make her shoes flash.

I shaded my eyes.

Back on the floor, Mrs. Roosevelt was everywhere. She darted to the red-faced kindergartner and plunked down a pair of sneakers with bunny laces, circled back to Alden, snatched away his makeshift skates, ignored his stuck-out tongue and shoved a pair of hockey-stick-patterned high-tops at him, took a deep breath, grimaced and shivered a little, then kicked the clown doll beneath a display counter.

"How are those feeling?" she asked the kindergartner.

The kindergartner's dad took out his wallet. "We'll take them."

A yes from Alden's mom too.

Only the little girl was left without new shoes. She was too traumatized by the clown to try any on.

The sales guy walked the customers to the cash register. His tie was crooked and his hair was a mess, but he was all smiles.

In no time flat, the crowd had cleared.

Mrs. Roosevelt tossed the shoehorn into the air with a little twirl, and handed it back to the still-grinning sales guy.

"How did you do that?" he asked breathlessly.

"Pish posh," replied Mrs. Roosevelt. "One merely needs to remain calm and focused. By doing so, any job can be accomplished . . . be it selling shoes or negotiating an international treaty."

"Still, it was a real *feet*." Olive giggled.

"You had to put your heart into it, body and *sole*," I added.

The sales guy groaned. "Shoe puns are painful. But give me some time and I'll *heel*."

Olive and I laughed.

"Won't you let me pay you for your time?" asked the sales guy.

"The satisfaction received from helping my fellow man is payment enough," replied Mrs. Roosevelt.

No kidding, she actually said that.

And it was pretty obvious she believed it too!

The sales guy pointed at the Princess Aquamarina Shimmer and Sparkle sneakers still flashing on Olive's feet. "At least let me give you the shoes."

Olive made one of her dolphin squeals. "Best birthday present ever!"

I blinked. Had her party really been just this morning? It felt like forever ago.

Mrs. Roosevelt was shaking her head. "That is very kind, but we cannot accept—"

"Dog!" shrieked Olive. She pointed out the window.

Fala was trotting down the sidewalk, sniffing the air, heading toward the Speedy Mart.

"Quick! Catch him!" I shouted.

"Thanks for the shoes, mister!" Olive shouted.

"I am so pleased to have been of assistance," Mrs. Roosevelt said.

We were already out the door when the sales guy hollered after Mrs. Roosevelt, "But I never caught your name. Who are you? You look so familiar!"

We didn't answer. Instead, we pounded down the sidewalk, Olive's new sneakers flashing bright enough to land planes in a fog.

## CHAPTER TEN

**I GOT TO THE** Speedy Mart first.

No Fala.

Panting, I put my hands on my hips. Geez, that dog was slippery. If somebody gave him one of those spit tests, I bet they'd find eel in his DNA.

"Hey, Nolan!" It was my buddy Alex Yee. He was coming out of the store carrying a Mega-Beast Big Swig Slushee... watermelon-lime, our favorite flavor. He grinned and was about to say something when Olive and Mrs. Roosevelt caught up.

*Flash! Blink! Twinkle!*

Three blinding bursts of light—purple, blue, green—blazed from Olive's feet.

Alex raised his arms to shield his face and stumbled backward. It was exactly what the vampire in this graphic novel *Stepson of Dracula* did when it saw the sun. Alex even *said* the same thing as the creature—"My eyes!"—as a twirling splat of watermelon-lime splashed red all over the front of his

White Sox T-shirt. In the graphic novel, it would have been blood.

"Ouch! That's gonna stain," said Olive.

Alex blinked a bunch of times and his face turned watermelon-red. "You could have blinded me!" he hollered at my sister.

She put her hand in front of his face, concerned. "How many fingers am I holding up?"

"And just look at my shirt!"

"Red looks good on you!"

Alex huffed and turned to me.

What could I say? I shrugged. "Sisters."

"Tell me about it." Alex rolled his eyes. He's got *three* of them at home. "Later, Nolan," he said in a disgusted voice. He squelched away.

I whirled on Olive.

"Those things are dangerous. You're a walking, talking, blinking accident waiting to happen. Can't you turn them off?"

She nodded. "Sure I can. But why would I want to? Watch!"

She started stomping and twirling.

*Flash-shimmer-flash-sparkle-flash!*

No kidding, it was like Tinker Bell threw up on Olive's feet.

Protecting her eyes with one gloved hand, Mrs. Roosevelt laid the other firmly on Olive's shoulder. "Nolan is right. Those shoes are a hazard. I must ask you to turn them off immediately."

Olive started to argue, but Mrs. Roosevelt snapped her fingers.

If you're smart, you never argue with a grown-up after she's finger-snapped, especially if that grown-up is the First Lady of the United States.

Olive bent and pressed the rhinestone

button on the back of each heel. The sneakers went dark . . . just like the crystal radio.

The radio! It felt like a hundred years since we'd left it sitting there, dark and lifeless, on the kitchen counter. We had to get back to it. Had to figure out what it wanted. Had to send Mrs. Roosevelt home. But first, we had to find Fala.

It didn't take long to search the Speedy Mart. Once we'd checked the area around the roller grill, peeked under the soft-serve machines, and strolled through the candy section, we'd pretty much seen it all.

Mrs. Roosevelt opened the dairy case and plucked out a squeezable tube. "This is *food*?"

Olive made a face. "No, yuck, that's yogurt." She picked up a bag of Freaky Fried Mac n' Cheesy Bacon Curds. "Now, *this* is food." She looked at me. "Buy me these, okay, Nolan?"

I ignored her. "This is a waste of time. Let's go."

"Before we do," said Mrs. Roosevelt, "perhaps we might pause and once again ask 'Where would a dog go?'"

"The park!" whooped Olive. She tossed the bag of curds back into the case.

Exasperated, I remarked, "That's where I said to look in the first place."

"Monkey bars, here I come!" whooped Olive.

"We're not playing," I reminded her. "We

have to find Fala so we can go home and . . ." I lowered my voice. "You know."

Olive turned suddenly serious. "Maybe we're *supposed* to swing on the monkey bars. Did you ever think of that, Nolan?" She was whispering now too. "Maybe Fala was *supposed* to run away. And I was *supposed* to get these awesome shoes and sizzle Alex's eyeballs. Maybe we're even supposed to buy that yummy bag of cheesy curds."

I frowned. "What are you talking about?"

"The radio," she said. "Remember all that stuff with Ben? How if we had just stayed at home and stared at the radio, we would never have learned what we needed to learn to send him back?"

I thought about that a moment. "You're right," I said.

"Again," she chirped, back to her usual annoying self.

The three of us headed for the door. But

as we came around the donut case, I stopped in my tracks.

What was *he* doing here?

And why was he always wearing that stupid trench coat?

The bats in my belly started going nuts. There could be only one reason for the snoopiest, sneakiest kid in town to be lurking in the magazine aisle.

"Are you *still* spying on us, Tommy?"

He put down the copy of *Chess and Checkers Weekly* he'd been pretending to read. He was all fake surprise and even faker smiles. "Oh, gee, it's Olive and Nolan Stanberry. Imagine bumping into you here!" He looked at the First Lady. "And what did you say your name was again?"

"She didn't," I said. Struggling to keep cool, I tightened my fists. "I mean it, Tommy. Stop following us."

"Me? Following you?" Tommy gave a fake little laugh. "I just came in for some . . . uh . . ."

His shifty eyes landed on a nearby display. "Whole Hog Bacon Jerky! Yeah, that's it. I came in for bacon jerky." He grabbed up two big handfuls of packages. "A guy can never have enough bacon jerky, you know?"

Olive and I watched him through narrowed eyes as he pushed some money at the bored teenager behind the counter. Then he shoved the meat strips into both trench coat pockets and gave me a little wave. "See you, Nolan."

"Not if I see you first," I replied. It wasn't a great line, I know. But I was nervous. I didn't like the sly look on Tommy's face.

"The best spies are *never* seen," he replied. "We're phantoms." And turning on his heel, he abruptly walked away.

"Big snoop head!" Olive hollered after him. She clasped her hands and turned to Mrs. Roosevelt. "Let me turn my shoes on him, pleeease!"

"It is tempting," said Mrs. Roosevelt.

"Fala," I reminded them.

We headed to the park.

# CHAPTER ELEVEN

**OUR TOWN PARK IS** smack-dab in the middle of Rolling Hills. Its official name is Casimir Pewey Park. Seriously. It's named for the town's founder. There's even a life-sized statue of the bushy-bearded Mr. Pewey next to the band shell. It looks like he has a bronze skunk on his face.

As we walked through the gate, Olive started singing that Rolling Hills first-grade classic: "Casimir Pewey eats chop suey for his Sunday meal. Eats too much and gets all spewy in the bookmobile."

Oh, brother!

"This is the park?" said Mrs. Roosevelt.

"It . . . it used to be," stammered Olive. She turned in a slow circle, pointing. "There was a playground over there. And benches under those trees. And the baseball diamond had bases." She shook her head. "Nolan, what happened?"

Yellow construction tape had been wound around the band shell to keep people out. The trellis in the rose garden had been removed. And the statue of Casmir Pewey had been swaddled in a cocoon of bubble wrap. It looked like an oversized knickknack on moving day. It even had a big yellow sticker slapped across its back end that read "Handle With Care."

"I don't know," I said.

Usually there were a gazillion people in the park—families having picnics and kids flying kites. But now it was empty except for a lone pigeon perched on Mr. Pewey's plastic-wrapped head, and two guys perched on their bulldozers in right field.

Olive's eyes started welling up. "Our park is gone."

"I suggest we find out why," said Mrs. Roosevelt. She strode briskly toward the bulldozers.

When the drivers saw her coming, they

climbed down. They were wearing orange coveralls with their names sewn on the pockets—Chuck and Buzz.

Mrs. Roosevelt stuck out one of her gloved hands.

Chuck shook it.

Buzz bared his teeth.

"May I ask what you gentlemen are doing here?" she asked.

Chuck answered, "We're going to bull-doze this place."

"Smash. Crash. Destroy," added Buzz gleefully. He showed his teeth again.

The guy was starting to scare me.

"But *whyyy*?" wailed Olive.

"To make room for a brand-spanking-new parking lot," said Chuck. "Seven hundred multiuse, state-of-the-art parking spaces."

I frowned. It didn't make sense. Were there even seven hundred cars in town?

"That's not right," I said. "Somebody should complain to the mayor, or whoever's in charge."

"*That* is an excellent idea, Nolan," said Mrs. Roosevelt.

"Save your breath," said Chuck. "The papers are signed. The ink's dry. It's a done deal. Tomorrow morning we—"

"Smash. Crash. Destroy," said Buzz.

Definitely scary.

Mrs. Roosevelt put her hands on her hips. "Then I must order you, as First Lady, to cease and desist at once."

Chuck laughed nastily. "First Lady of what? The loony bin?"

"Of the United States, you meanie!" cried Olive.

I hid my face behind my hands and groaned.

Buzz laughed too, and his eyes swept over Mrs. Roosevelt, taking in her white tennis shoes and goofy hairnet. "First Lady? You? Hardly."

Mrs. Roosevelt huffed. "I will have you know that my name has been at the top of the Best-Dressed List for three years running."

The drivers cracked up at that. Chuck laughed so hard he fell over in the dirt. When he got ahold of himself, he said, "You know, you *do* look familiar." He nudged Buzz. "Don't she look familiar?"

Buzz squinted. "Maybe we've seen her at Miss Bea's Teas?"

"Time to go!" I cried, taking Mrs. Roosevelt's arm.

She wouldn't budge. "I have yet to finish my conversation with these gentlemen."

"Fala," I reminded her.

"Fala?" asked Chuck. "What's a Fala?"

"Our lost dog," blurted Olive.

"Awwww," said Buzz , his face turning all

soft and rubbery. "I lost my Scruffy when I was ten, and—"

"Haven't seen no dogs," Chuck butted in. "But the animal control office is in the town hall. And that's conveniently *not* located in this park, if you catch my drift."

I looked at Olive, and she looked at Mrs.

Roosevelt, and we all said at the same time, "The town hall!"

We were halfway to the gate when Buzz yelled after us. "Hope you find your pooch!"

# CHAPTER TWELVE

**FALA WAS SITTING ON** the marble steps of the town hall. I'm not kidding. It was like he was waiting for us or something. When he saw us coming around the corner, he trotted right over and gave us a look that said, "Here I am. What took you so long?"

Olive couldn't stop hugging and kissing him. "Oh, Fala baby, Fala baby," she squealed. "We found you. You're here. You're safe. *Mwah! Mwah! Mwah!*"

It was pretty embarrassing.

Mrs. Roosevelt was happy to see Fala too. Even though she just ruffled his ears and said, "You naughty rascal," I heard the crack in her voice. Then she bent low over his head to hide her face and swiped a tear from the corner of her eye. I guess she'd been more worried than she let on.

I don't mean to sound sappy or anything, but my heart did a little dance when Fala finally escaped from Olive's kisses long enough to put his front paws on my knees. I wanted to yell at him for running away and not listening and making us all worry. But when the little guy wiggled and smiled his funny dog smile by curling back his lip to show his teeth, I just sort of melted. "Come on, buddy," I said to him. "Let's go home."

"Not until we've spoken with the mayor," said Mrs. Roosevelt.

"Oh, no," I said, shaking my head so hard I thought it might come off. "No, no, that is *not* a good idea. We cannot get involved. Someone might recognize you."

Olive rolled her eyes. "Noooo one ever recognizes her."

I tried a different argument. "Didn't you hear Chuck and Buzz? The mayor's already made up her mind. We can't fight city hall. It's done."

"It is only done if you do nothing," said Mrs. Roosevelt.

"So true," said Olive. "Tell him, Ellie."

"Mrs. Roosevelt," Mrs. Roosevelt corrected her. She turned back to me.

"It is not just the *right* of Americans to speak up. It is our *duty*."

"Hey, that makes me want to sing!" Olive exclaimed. She clapped her hand over her heart and began belting out "The

Star-Spangled Banner." *"Ooooh-kay, can you seeeee? By the red parts we washed . . ."*

Obviously, she was still learning the words.

"Democracy is not about words. It is about action."

*"And the monkey's red hair. The plums bursting in air . . ."*

"This is no ordinary time, Nolan. We must do what is best for this town. This community. This country."

*"And the hooome of the paraaaade!"*

"All right, already. I give up."

"Play ball!" she cried.

We pushed open the town hall's big double doors and stepped into its cool darkness. The mayor's office was two doors down on the right.

Closed For
Mayor Selff's
Construction
Party
WHOOP!!!

"Uh-oh," said Olive.

For a second we just stood there, letting it sink in.

Then Olive made a face. "This stinks!"

"It certainly does," agreed Mrs. Roosevelt. "Monday will be too late."

I felt a pinch of sadness. The park shouldn't be plowed over. But what more could we do?

"I guess that's that," I said.

Mrs. Roosevelt shook her head. "We cannot give up so easily. There must be some solution. We have only to think of it."

"Yeah, well, let's think about it back at home, okay?" I said.

We crossed Main Street, Fala trotting obediently beside us like a well-trained show dog. We turned the corner. Rolling Hills Middle School came into view.

Olive shaded her eyes. "Hey, isn't that your team out there on the field, Nolan?"

"Pavlov's Pest Control?"

The soccer league uses the school's field.

Coach Filbert's voice drifted across the field. "Pass it! Pass it!" Obviously, my team

126

was getting in a little practice before tomorrow afternoon's game against Fred and Ethel's Cleaning Service.

I ducked behind Mrs. Roosevelt. "Uh . . . er . . . no," I stammered.

"Sure it is," insisted Olive. "I can see the little cockroach on the backs of their uniforms. Hey, how come you're not out there with them?"

I jerked my chin toward Mrs. Roosevelt. "Something more important popped up, remember?"

But that wasn't the *whole* reason.

I peeked around the First Lady.

Out on the field, the new kid on the team, Heather Lynne, double-scissor-stepped down the field and blasted an arcing shot that hung in the air just long enough for the entire team to gasp before it landed in the goal.

For a kid, Heather is the best soccer player I've ever seen.

She makes me feel like the worst.

I'd never felt that way until two weeks earlier, when she'd turned up to play on the team.

"So, Heather Lynne," C. J. McCabe said, smirking, that first day. "What makes you think you've got the moves to play with the Pests?"

"Well, I was the striker on my last team," she'd replied matter-of-factly.

Eloise Dunlop elbowed me in the ribs. "Sounds like she's after *your* position, Nolan."

*Not if I can help it,* I thought.

C.J.'s smirk grew bigger. "Let's show her who's really got the moves, huh, Stanberry?"

Coach threw the ball in the air.

*Thwup!*

I bounced it off my knee the way my dad had taught me. Before the divorce, we used to practice our moves in the backyard all the time.

"Nice," Denzel Sweeney said.

I puffed up my chest. Dad would have been proud.

The ball landed on the ground, but before I could get to it, Heather made a deadly pivot kick that shot past me.

"She's fast, Stanberry!" called out Giancarlo Cuellar.

"Yeah, Nolan, better watch out!" added Eugene Stickney.

I charged after the ball.

"Girls rule!" yelled Eloise.

*Oh, no they don't!* I shouted in my head. *Out of my way, Heather!*

"Good hustle, Stanberry!" shouted the coach.

Cutting to the center, I hoofed the ball toward the goal, then wound my leg back for a cannonball kick and . . . missed. My legs flew out from under me. A second later, my butt was in the grass.

C.J. held his stomach and busted out laughing. "You . . . you . . . *fanny* flopped!"

I gritted my teeth, the bats flapping away in my belly.

Heather strolled over and stuck out her hand. "Need help up?" she asked in a calm voice.

"No, I do *not* need your stupid help!" Smacking her hand away, I stood. This was it. If I didn't prove my moves now, Coach would make her the team striker.

Huffing and puffing, I ran at the ball again. But Heather just back-heeled it between my legs, then stepped on it. She looked at me, her face set and determined. "Ready?" she said. I knew there was no stopping her. It was in her eyes: she was going to slam it into my chest. She lifted her foot to kick the ball.

I ducked and covered.

And Heather tapped the ball to Denzel.

He booted it into the net.

"Goal!" cried Coach Filbert.

C.J. went into another fit of hysterics.

By this time I felt totally sick. All I could do was watch as my teammates and Heather began practicing passes, shouting and calling to one another. And . . . this is sort of hard to explain, but I swear I felt myself shrinking.

Turning into a teensy-weensy nobody on the team. And it was all hotshot Heather Lynne's fault.

Anyway, that was the real reason I was hiding behind the First Lady.

"Please, *pleeease* don't let anyone from my team notice me," I mumbled to myself.

Just then, Olive started shouting. "GOOOOO, PESTS!"

Geez, could she be any more obvious?

She waved her arms wildly and hopped up and down. "KICK IT! KICK IT! KICK IT!"

Yes, she could.

Heather Lynne turned and spied me hiding behind Mrs. Roosevelt. She raised a hand in the air.

I closed my eyes and wished the ground would open up and swallow me.

As usual, the ground didn't.

I had to get away. Grabbing Olive's flapping arm, I tried to drag her back the way we'd come. It wasn't easy. Olive is squirmy.

"Lemme go!" she hollered, shaking off my hand.

Mrs. Roosevelt stepped between us and put her hands on her hips. "What is all this tussling about?"

"Olive won't go home," I said. My voice sounded nervous and squeaky. I could feel Heather Lynne's eyes boring into me from across the soccer field.

"But *that's* not the way home," said Olive. She pointed across the field. "*This* is."

"My way is . . . um . . . uh . . . a shortcut," I said.

"No it's not," she said.

"Just come on, okay, Olive?" I said through clenched teeth.

Mrs. Roosevelt looked at me curiously. Then she said, "Let us go where Nolan leads."

"But it's waaay out of the way," whined Olive.

Mrs. Roosevelt snapped her fingers.

"Lead on, Nolan," said Olive.

We were turning the corner onto Sherwood Lane when I bent and pretended to tie my shoe. I glanced at Heather out of the corner of my eye.

She was bouncing the soccer ball off her head.

I felt myself shrink a little more. Basically, I was the size of a raisin.

## CHAPTER THIRTEEN

**I DON'T GO DOWN** Sherwood Lane too often, mostly because none of my friends live there. Most all the houses on the street are made of brick and have two stories and these giant porches that go almost the whole way around. I guess that's why Rolling Hills calls it the historic district. I just call it old.

Fala trotted ahead to pee on stuff— a picket fence, an oak tree, a sign with bulldozer-shaped helium balloons tied to it.

From the house came sounds of laughter and conversation.

Mrs. Roosevelt stopped in her tracks and stared.

I knew what she was thinking. "Nuh-uh. Oh, no. We can't," I said.

"We must," she replied.

"What are you guys talking about?" asked Olive.

"We can't just waltz into the mayor's party uninvited," I insisted.

"Another party?" squealed Olive. "Two in

one day? Oooh, I hope the mayor serves those little meatballs. You know, the ones wrapped in bacon? Mmmm, I love meatballs with bacon."

*"Arrr-woof,"* said Fala.

"We cannot crash this party!" I said again.

We crashed the mayor's party.

Although, to be honest, there was no crashing involved. We all just walked in through her open front door. Even Fala.

The place was crammed with grown-ups,

standing around and balancing little plates of toothpick-speared appetizers.

"Bacon meatballs!" exclaimed Olive.

*"Arrrf!"* barked Fala.

They raced for the refreshment table.

Right away, I spotted Mrs. Bustamante, the library director. She was chatting with Mr. Treble from the music store and Ms. Lacy, owner of Tattoo You. The Long John

Shivers ice cream guy was there too, although it took a second for me to recognize him. I'd never seen him without his eye patch before.

I grabbed Mrs. Roosevelt's arm. "There aren't any kids here."

"Act like you belong, and no one will doubt you," she replied.

To prove her point, she turned to Mrs. Delacruz, president of the bank. "How lovely to see you," gushed Mrs. Roosevelt.

Mrs. Delacruz gasped. "You . . . you have a spider on your forehead."

"It is a hairnet," explained Mrs. Roosevelt.

"I like it," said Mrs. Krosoczka.

Mrs. Krosoczka is the school lunch lady.

"Can you tell me where I might find your hostess?" Mrs. Roosevelt asked.

"Mayor Selff?" The lunch lady scanned the crowded room. "She's around here somewhere. . . ."

"Citizens of Rolling Hills!"

"Oh, right there!"

At the front of the room, a dark-haired woman wearing a red, white, and blue sweater with a matching navy skirt shouted to get everyone's attention.

"She looks like a flag," Olive said through meatball-greasy lips. "She looks like the Fourth of July."

"*Arrrf!*" said Fala. He'd been giving Olive the Treatment. And it was working. I could tell by the bits of bacon in his whiskers.

"What a joy it is to see the civic and business leaders of our fair community gathered together for this celebration of growth and change," said the mayor. She pumped a fist in the air. "Progress is now!"

Beside me, Mrs. Roosevelt muttered, "Stuff and nonsense."

"Can I get some more meatballs?" asked Olive.

Fala licked his chops.

"Tomorrow morning at ten o'clock we will break ground at Pewey Park in a public ceremony," continued the mayor. "I hope all of you will be there to witness the historic moment when Rolling Hills steps into the future."

"But what about the present?" Mrs.

Roosevelt called out. "What about today's needs for fresh air, exercise, and recreation?"

The guests murmured and started shuffling their feet, like they were suddenly uncomfortable.

"Who said that?" asked the mayor.

I put out my hand to stop her, but Mrs. Roosevelt pushed her way to the front of the room. "I did, Madam Mayor. I have come to speak with you about this parking lot business."

Mayor Selff frowned. "Do I know you?"

Mrs. Roosevelt shook her head. "We've never met. Still, I—"

"So you're a party crasher!" exclaimed Mayor Selff.

I groaned. I knew it. This was a bad idea. A very bad idea.

Mayor Selff beckoned to someone in the back of the room. "Officer Nittles, this woman is trespassing. Kindly escort her to the door."

*Not* Officer Nittles! She was the police-woman who'd driven Olive and me home after our . . . um . . . little stunt involving Ben Franklin and a fire truck. Geez, she was going to think I was a juvenile delinquent or something.

Officer Nittles moved toward the First Lady.

Mrs. Roosevelt raised her chin. "I will *not* be silenced."

"Hear her out!" someone shouted. An old guy with white hair and a cane shuffled forward.

"Really, Dad?" said the mayor with an exasperated sigh. "You're taking *her* side?"

He moved closer to stare into Mrs. Roosevelt's face. Then he turned to the mayor. "I think you should listen to this woman, Darlene. I believe she will have something extraordinary to say."

"Fine," said the mayor, sounding like a sulky teenager. "But make it quick."

"I shall do my best," said Mrs. Roosevelt. She faced the crowd. "Friends," she began, her voice fluttering. "Sometimes change is not the important thing. Sometimes we need to appreciate what we already have."

The crowd stirred, then quieted and leaned forward to listen.

"Allow me to tell you a story," she said.

And just like before, her words formed pictures in my head.

It was 1939, but not once had an English king or queen ever set foot on American soil.

Until now.

Read all about it!

The country buzzed with excitement. Here was our chance to impress the royal couple.

And let's host a sumptuous twelve-course feast. We can serve escargot and caviar and peacocks. You know, royal-people food.

And a ball. A magnificent, fairy-tale-type ball.

You need a crown. Shall we call Tiffany's?

Actually, I had thought to celebrate the royal visit with an all-American hot dog picnic at our family home in Hyde Park.

My idea, when newspapers reported it, was not a popular one.

Thousands of letters poured in from all over the country.

I responded by writing about it in my daily newspaper column.

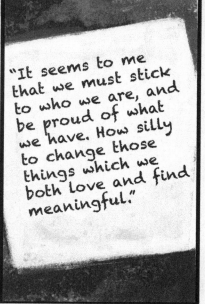

"It seems to me that we must stick to who we are, and be proud of what we have. How silly to change those things which we both love and find meaningful."

The day of the picnic arrived, a lovely June afternoon ...

... perfect weather for a picnic with ...

... two hundred and fifty guests ...

... and King George and Queen Elizabeth of England.

Lunch was served.

How *do* I *eat* this?

Just push it in your mouth and keep pushing until it's gone.

King George picked one up with his fingers. After a moment he gobbled it down, licked his lips, and . . .

. . . asked for seconds.

The queen was less enthusiastic.

Still, a good time was had by all. And a lasting friendship between the royals and the Roosevelts was forged.

I was surprised at what a good storyteller Mrs. Roosevelt was. I guess just because a person wears a hairnet doesn't mean she's totally boring. So it was strange that only Olive and I clapped when she finished. The mayor's father showed his appreciation too. He put his fingers in his mouth and whistled like a train. I have to admit, it was pretty impressive.

"Honestly, Dad, get a grip," said the mayor. She flashed a fake smile at Mrs. Roosevelt. "Thank you for that ... er ... interesting story. But sentiment cannot be allowed to stand in the way of progress. Rolling Hills is a little town with a big future. Progress starts now." She started chanting, "Progress! Progress! Progress!"

Her dad's expression was stony, like he would have grounded her if he could. Too bad the mayor was so ancient. I bet she was at least thirty.

Out of the corner of my eye, I saw

Officer Nittles coming toward me. I snaked my way to the front of the room. "I think we should go," I said to Mrs. Roosevelt.

"Indeed, there is nothing more to be done here," she agreed.

We headed for the door.

"Hold up a sec!" cried Olive. She snagged a couple more meatballs off the refreshment table.

We were already on the front porch when the mayor's dad called out, "Wait a moment, won't you?" He trundled out after us. "I want to thank you for your inspirational words . . . *Mrs. Roosevelt.*"

"Hey, somebody does recognize you!" Olive piped up.

Oh, geez, no, this could not be happening. I stammered, "Er . . . uh . . . you've made a mistake. This is our . . . um . . . babysitter."

He shook his head. "Anyone who's ever met Eleanor Roosevelt couldn't possibly forget her."

The First Lady took his wrinkled hand in her gloved one. "We've met?"

He nodded. "You were older than you are now. It was 1959, and you spoke at my high school graduation ceremony. Afterward, I was lucky enough to have my picture taken with you. It was one of the greatest days of my life."

"I hope you will forgive me for not remembering," said Mrs. Roosevelt. "Your graduation day is still years in my future."

He nodded his understanding.

Oh, no, no, no, no, no! "I . . . I . . . think you're confused," I said to the mayor's dad. "That's not—"

"I know what I know, young fella," he said. "That is Eleanor Roosevelt. How she got here and why she came remain mysteries, but 'there are more things in heaven and earth, Horatio . . .'"

Horatio again? Who *was* that guy?

Fala made a weird noise.

The mayor's dad went on. "I've lived a long time, and with age comes wisdom. I know the impossible is possible. But don't worry." He laid a hand on my shoulder. "I won't tell a soul who she really is. Heck, folks would say I'd gone senile if I did."

And here's the crazy thing. I looked up into his kind brown eyes and . . . I don't know why . . . but I believed him. I truly did.

"And what is your name, sir?" asked Mrs. Roosevelt.

"Howard Selff," he replied with a salute.

Fala made another weird noise.

Mayor Selff came out onto the porch. "Are you still chatting with these party crashers? Honestly, Dad!"

Just then, Fala walked over to where the mayor was standing and threw up on her shoe.

"Oopsies," said Olive. "Too many meatballs."

## CHAPTER FOURTEEN

**AFTER THE MAYOR SLAMMED** the door in our faces, Mrs. Roosevelt wheeled around and strode briskly down the sidewalk. The First Lady, I was discovering, didn't do anything at old lady speed. Olive and I practically had to run to keep up.

It didn't take long to get home. In the kitchen, the crystal radio still sat on the counter, dark and silent. I groaned. I'd been hoping the radio would turn on when we walked in the door.

The three of us peered down at it for a few long moments.

"I guess we didn't learn anything today," I finally said.

"Stuff and nonsense," replied Mrs. Roosevelt. "We learn by living. Every day is an opportunity to make discoveries."

"Like you can't call Mrs. Roosevelt Ellie," Olive piped up.

"Precisely," said Mrs. Roosevelt.

"And that Scotties and meatballs don't mix," added Olive.

Mrs. Roosevelt nodded.

"And that clown dolls are really scary."

I ignored her and turned to Mrs. Roosevelt. "But we didn't learn the *right* things. The things that will send you back."

"Then we shall continue living and learning until we do," said the First Lady.

"What about the park?" asked Olive.

"We shall keep fighting for it, naturally."

"We're not quitting?" I said.

"To quit would be to abandon our principles," declared Mrs. Roosevelt. "No, Nolan, we must raise our voices even louder. We must protest . . . at tomorrow's groundbreaking ceremony."

A knot formed in my stomach.

"P-p-protest?" I stuttered. "Honest, Mrs. Roosevelt, I don't think kids are allowed to do that."

"All Americans—even children—have the right to peacefully protest," she replied.

"Huh?" said Olive. "Who says?"

"The United States Constitution," Mrs. Roosevelt replied

"No way! Really?" Olive let out one of her dolphin squeals. "Ooooh, I *love* protesting. I'm supergood at it too. Listen." She started shouting. "No, I will not pick up my mermaid dolls! No, I will not brush my teeth! No, I will not eat those garbanzo beans!"

Oh, brother!

Mrs. Roosevelt smiled. "The Constitution only gives people the right to protest against their government, Olive, not against their parents."

Olive put her hands on her hips. "Whose stupid idea was that?"

"The Founding Fathers'," said Mrs. Roosevelt.

"Which would include Ben Franklin," I added.

Olive shook her head sadly. "Oh, Benny, why? *Why?*"

"Even if it's not against the law, we shouldn't be protesting tomorrow," I went on. "Think about it. There will be lots of people at the groundbreaking ceremony. What if somebody else recognizes Mrs. Roosevelt? You know, somebody like Tommy Tuttle or Officer Nittles? Somebody who can't keep a secret?"

"But we have to live and learn, Nolan," Olive said.

I hesitated. "I don't know. . . ."

*Buh-dop!* My phone interrupted my thoughts.

I picked it up off the counter.

Tomorrow night? The knot in my stomach grew bigger. Oh, geez, Mom would be home tomorrow night! In all the craziness, she'd slipped my mind. I ran my hands through my hair. Tomorrow night. Mrs.

Roosevelt and Fala had to be gone by then, or else. . . . I groaned. I had no choice.

I turned to the First Lady. "Let's protest," I said.

\* \* \*

Mrs. Roosevelt became a whirlwind of activity. Pacing the room, she began tapping her forehead with her gloved finger. Every tap seemed to knock out another idea.

"Signs and posters. We shall need dozens of signs and posters."

*Tap-tap!*

"And a speech."

*Tap-tap!*

"Most importantly, we must get the word out. How can citizens join our protest if they are unaware of it?"

She stopped pacing and looked at the wall clock: eight-thirty. "It is already so late." She sighed. "If only there were a fast way to contact hundreds of people within minutes."

Olive grinned. "Ellie," she said, "have I got a surprise for you."

Before Mrs. Roosevelt could correct her, Olive grabbed the First Lady's arm and led her into the computer room. She started typing.

I looked at the screen.

Who knew my little sister had her own Kidschat page?

I did a double take.

Or that she had so many followers?

"The Princess of Norway?" I exclaimed.

Olive shrugged. "What can I say? I post regularly, and my content is interesting." She clicked a few more keys.

I had to hand it to Mrs. Roosevelt. She grasped the basics of social media pretty quickly. She especially liked Twitter. "Oh, I wish Franklin and I had such a wonderful means of communication. Just imagine the morale-boosting messages we could send to the American people!"

We brainstormed for a few minutes and finally came up with this post:

Olive added pictures of a bulldozer, an abandoned park, and mermaid Princess Aquamarina.

"Are you sure about the mermaid?" I asked.

"Trust me, Nolan," she said. "It's all about grabbing attention."

I nodded. If anyone knew about that, it was Olive.

"There's just one last thing," she said. She clicked even more keys. "I'm adding a link to my website. We can put even more stuff about us protesting there."

"You have a *website*?" I said. "Does Mom know?"

"Of course," replied Olive with a roll of her eyes. "She monitors it every day."

"Geez, I hope she sends *me* to technology day camp next summer," I said.

While Olive put the final touches on her website—more pictures of mermaids, along with puppies and something she called a chimera—"Part lion, part goat, part snake!"—I went up to Mom's studio for colored markers and cardboard.

Then the three of us sat around the dining room table and tried to come up

with ideas for our protest signs. Sure, Olive
has computer know-how, but I'm pretty
good at art. I think it's because of all the
graphic novels I read. Anyway, I started
doodling, and in no time at all, I hit on
this idea:

"Imaginative," said Mrs. Roosevelt. She
held up her poster. "What do you think
of mine?"

"Er . . . nice handwriting," I said.

"Look at mine! Look at mine!" cried Olive.

"But it's not quite finished." Olive picked up a brown marker.

"Oh, no you don't," I said, snatching it out of her hand.

"What?" said Olive. "I just wanted to color in her eyes."

*Yeah, right.*

We worked for a long time.

Then Olive let out a huge yawn and . . . *Thump!* Just like that, her head dropped to the table.

I reached over to shake her.

"Do not disturb her," said Mrs. Roosevelt. "I will carry her up."

I must have looked doubtful, because she added, "As a regular practitioner of yoga, I am stronger than I look." And before I could say another word, she did this.

And this.

And this.

Then she picked up Olive. For a moment her features softened as she looked at my sister's sleeping face. "Sweet," said Mrs. Roosevelt.

A string of saliva oozed from the corner of Olive's mouth.

"Not," I said.

Mrs. Roosevelt looked at me. "You need to get some sleep too, Nolan. Remember, with the new day comes new strength and new thoughts."

With a yawn, I followed her up the stairs.

## CHAPTER FIFTEEN

**IT WAS STILL DARK** when the doorbell rang. Blurry-eyed, I looked at my bedside clock: five-thirty.

With a groan, I stumbled out into the hallway.

Olive came out of her room too. "What's happening?"

Mrs. Roosevelt looked up at us from the entry hall. "Good morning, children!" she chirped. She looked wide-awake and brimming with energy. Even her hairnet was neatly in place. "Look who's here. . . . Mr. Selff!"

"At this hour?" I croaked.

"I saw your post on Kidschat and I came to help."

"You're on Kidschat?" said Olive.

"My grandkids are," he replied.

"Well, we are thrilled that you have joined our ranks," said Mrs. Roosevelt. "And you are just in time for breakfast. Will you stay? I cooked."

We all went into the kitchen and sat down at the table.

"Where's Fala?" I asked.

"Hiding," said Mrs. Roosevelt. She clattered some pots and pans on the stove. "As I said, I cooked."

Mr. Selff and I exchanged worried looks, and Mrs. Roosevelt started spooning food onto our plates.

"Scrambled eggs with tomato sauce," she said.

"Poached prunes."

"Prunes will give you a real run for your money," said Mr. Selff.

"And . . ."

"Gross!" exclaimed Olive. "What's that?"

"Mashed potatoes on a slice of whole-wheat bread."

The three of us stared at our plates.

"It is a seven-and-a-half-cent breakfast," declared Mrs. Roosevelt.

"Overpriced," I muttered.

Mrs. Roosevelt looked indignant. "I will have you know that I devised this meal myself. It is inexpensive as well as nutritious."

I poked at the prunes with my fork. "You and President Roosevelt don't actually eat this stuff yourselves, do you?"

"Of course we do," replied Mrs. Roosevelt. "There is a Great Depression going on."

"A Great Impression?" said Olive.

"*De*pression," I corrected her. "Back in the 1930s, lots and lots of people were out of work because the economy crashed. It seemed like everybody was poor, or hungry, or homeless."

Mrs. Roosevelt nodded. "Well told, Nolan. That is exactly right."

I blushed. Geez. My teacher, Mr. Druff, would never believe it.

"How come you and Frankie eat this stuff?" Olive said, wrinkling her nose. "You're not poor, are you?"

"It is President Roosevelt," Mrs. Roosevelt corrected her. "And no, we are not poor. But Franklin and I believe it would be wrong to dine on seven-course meals while our fellow citizens stand in soup-kitchen lines."

A guy had to admire that, even if it did mean eating slop. Picking up my fork, I poked at the tomato-drippy eggs. Disgusting! Still, there were people starving back in Mrs. Roosevelt's time. I put a tiny bite in my mouth. Chewed. Swallowed. Covered my mouth and tried not to gag.

"They're not *so* bad," I lied. But no way was I touching those prunes.

Mrs. Roosevelt sat down. She smiled at Mr. Selff. "I am just so pleased you are with us."

"You can carry a sign at the protest,"

added Olive. "Or . . . wait! You can hand out candy!"

"It's a protest, not a parade, doofus," I said. "Nobody's handing out candy."

"Make balloon animals, then?" asked Olive.

Mr. Selff chuckled. "All those jobs sound like fun, little miss. But I had something a bit different in mind."

The sudden twinkle in his eyes made me uneasy.

"Like what?" I asked.

"Like flying the plane," he replied.

## CHAPTER SIXTEEN

**IT TURNED OUT MR.** Selff had been a crop duster before he retired, which means he knew how to swoop, and dive, and . . .

"Skywrite," he said. "What better way to advertise your rally than to write *big*—big enough for everyone who isn't online to see?"

"Who isn't online?" asked Olive. She shot me a smug look.

I ignored her and thought about Mr. Selff's suggestion. It was pretty good. *Everyone* reads skywriting. I mean, who can resist a puffy white message stretched across a clear blue sky? It's even more of an attention grabber than Olive.

"When are you going to do it?" I asked.

"Right now," he said, slapping his hands on the table and standing. "The sun should just about be up by the time we get to the airstrip."

"You mean *you*," I corrected him. "By the time *you* get to the airstrip."

"I can't very well fly without a copilot." He smiled knowingly at Mrs. Roosevelt.

She smiled back.

Olive looked from one to the other. Then she burst out, "You can fly, Ellie? Wow! Are there even planes back in your time?"

"Mrs. Roosevelt," retorted Mrs. Roosevelt. "And yes, of course there are airplanes. It is true that airline travel is in its infancy. Still, I am a stalwart advocate." She stood too. "I am ready when you are, Mr. Selff. And the children, I believe, will enjoy the experience."

"Um ... I—I think I'll just stay here,"

I stammered, "and . . . uh . . . finish these, uh, delicious eggs."

"Absolutely not," Mrs. Roosevelt replied in a firm voice. "You and Olive are my responsibility while your mother is away. I will not shirk my duty by leaving you alone." She snapped her fingers.

I went upstairs to get dressed.

As I was pulling on my shorts and T-shirt, Fala poked his head out from under my bed.

"You better stay hidden," I warned him, "or Mrs. Roosevelt will make you go up too."

Fala whined.

"I know. I hate heights. Seriously, stand-ing on a step stool makes me dizzy."

*"Arrr-woof!"* barked Fala, as if he agreed. He scooted back under the bed.

I dragged myself into the bathroom. Just the thought of soaring hundreds of feet above the ground was making me queasy. I opened the medicine cabinet, took out a bottle of Pepto-Bismol, and downed a swig. After that, I ate two Tums and shuffled downstairs and out the door. I crawled into the backseat of Mr. Selff's gold Buick.

"And we're off!" cried Mr. Selff. Gripping the steering wheel with both hands, he inched out onto Kenton Street, then oh-so-carefully maneuvered the car around the corner onto Harrison Road. We crawled out of town.

Olive cupped her mouth and whispered in my ear, "And I thought Great-Aunt Mildred drove slow. I sure hope he flies better than he drives."

I burped. Eggs and Tums. Gross!

Keeping his eyes glued to the road, Mr. Selff asked, "When was the last time you were up, Mrs. Roosevelt?"

"In a private plane?" she replied. "Oh, I have not done that since I flew with Amelia."

"Earhart?" I gasped.

"The one and only," replied Mrs. Roosevelt.

"I'd like to hear about that," said Mr. Selff.

"Me too," I said.

"Me three," added Olive.

Mrs. Roosevelt smiled. "It appears I have a story to tell."

And as she spoke, pictures filled my mind.

There are few things I love more than flying.

I love the magical, weightless feeling of leaving the earth behind.

I love the expanse and beauty of our country as seen from above.

And I love the speed with which I can travel from one city to the next.

Sadly, few Americans share my passion.

But *she* did.

She was the first female pilot to fly solo across the Atlantic Ocean.

The first female pilot to fly solo from coast to coast without a single stop.

The first female pilot to fly solo from Mexico to New Jersey.

She was Amelia Earhart, my dear friend.

And my dinner guest.

Of course we talked about flying.

Honestly, Eleanor, there's nothing as glorious as a night flight.

It is too bad commercial airlines are restricted to daytime flying. How I would love to experience flight in the dark!

I shall never understand choosing dessert over adventure.

What a clear, lovely night it was for flying.

The world below me looked both familiar and unfamiliar, luminous and twinkling, a fairyland I had never imagined existed.

Stars. Planets. Moonlight on the clouds below. The engine hummed. So did my heart.

When Amelia offered me the controls, I did not hesitate for an instant.

Was I afraid? Not at all. I had the world's finest pilot beside me.

The finest friend, too.

It was past midnight when we got back. Everyone was asleep.

Oh, how I miss Amelia.

Mrs. Roosevelt fell silent after that. So did we. No one spoke until we inched onto the airstrip—a single runway carved out of the middle of a cornfield. A rusty hangar stood off to one side. Parked in front of it were two airplanes. One looked like something that had actually been around since Amelia Earhart's time—all beat-up and covered with rust spots. The other one was sleek and modern. Its silver shone like a diamond in the early-morning light.

We climbed out of the car and followed Mr. Selff as he hobbled over to the second plane.

I felt myself relax a little. At least his plane looked safe.

He patted one of its shiny wings. "I just don't see the need for these fancy ladies," he said. He turned to the rust bucket. "Now, this old gal may not have all the modern geegaws, but she can still get the job done. I tell you, she's a real workhorse."

Mrs. Roosevelt smiled. "She and I have much in common."

Mr. Selff opened the small door of the old-timey plane. I poked my head inside and froze. This was it? Just four seats—two in front and two in back—crammed into a tiny tube of metal? Nuh-uh. No way. I was NOT getting in.

Olive shoved me from behind, then clambered in after me.

Mrs. Roosevelt took the front passenger seat.

"This is soooo cool!" squealed Olive.

I burped up another taste of Tums.

It took Mr. Selff a few minutes to climb into the pilot's seat, what with his cane and stiff knees and all. Then he took a long, careful look at the controls, pushed a few buttons, and played with some pedals on the floor. At last, the engine sputtered and the propeller started whirling.

"Here we go," he said, moving the control stick.

The airplane taxied down the runway, picking up speed bit by bit.

"Whoopee!" shrieked Olive. She raised her hands above her head like she was on a roller coaster. "Isn't this fun, Nolan?"

I put my hand over my mouth as my stomach lurched. I could feel every dip and bump on the runway as we roared over it, faster and faster, until . . .

"We're flying! We're flying!" crowed Olive.

My heart lodged in my throat as we went up . . . up . . . up.

Mr. Selff banked the plane right, and I
looked down at the airfield and watched the
hangar getting smaller and smaller until it
looked like a toy. Staying beneath the clouds,
we leveled out, and Rolling Hills came into
view. I recognized the library and the town
hall and Pewey Park with the bulldozers still
waiting at the edge of the baseball diamond.

"Look, there's our house!" hollered Olive.
A second later she added, "And is that ...
Tommy Tuttle?"

It was. I'd recognize that trench coat
anywhere. He was going from window to

window and peering in. I burped again. There was only one reason for Tommy to be lurking around my house. I thought of the crystal radio sitting out in the open on the kitchen counter. Why hadn't I taken the time to hide it? I knew from experience that Tommy wasn't above sneaking into people's homes.

I pounded on the airplane window. "Get away, snoop!" I hollered, even though I knew Tommy couldn't hear me.

"Problem, son?" shouted Mr. Selff above the roar of the engine.

I pointed.

"Ah, Tuttle trouble!" he said.

"You know him?" shouted Olive.

"Everybody knows the Tuttles!" Mr. Selff shouted back, like that explained it. Which, actually, it did.

Circling the plane back around, he came in lower.

We could see Tommy clearly now. As we passed overhead, he whirled and pressed his binoculars to his eyes. A second later, his mouth dropped open and his eyebrows rose all the way to his bushy hairline.

"Buzz him! Buzz him!" shrieked Olive.

"Problems are never solved by buzzing!" Mrs. Roosevelt shouted.

"But we're too far away to slug him!" Olive shouted back.

Below, Tommy hopped on his bike and

took off pedaling. I didn't like the determined look on his face.

Then Mr. Selff banked again. In moments, we were past the town and flying higher over a sea of corn and soybeans.

"Take the controls, Mrs. Roosevelt!" he shouted.

A confident smile spread across the First Lady's face as she gripped the stick.

I clutched my seat belt, all thoughts of Tommy evaporating. I braced myself for stomach-churning bucking and bumping.

But Mrs. Roosevelt flew smoothly. I almost started to relax and enjoy the scenery.

Then Mr. Selff shouted, "Reach on up here and give it a whirl, son!"

*"What?"*

"Reach up here and take the control stick!" he shouted again.

"I . . . I can't."

"Whyever not?" shouted Mrs. Roosevelt.

"You must do the thing you think you cannot do."

I shook my head.

"Life is meant to be lived, Nolan. Seize the day!" she shouted.

"Seize it!" shouted Olive.

"Don't be afraid. You can handle her!" shouted Mr. Selff.

I still don't know where I found the nerve to do it. But quickly, before I had a chance to think about it, I leaned forward—my seat belt digging into my hips—and grasped the stick just above Mrs. Roosevelt's hand. For a moment, both of us were steering the plane.

Then she let go.

And I was flying—actually, truly flying—an airplane.

My hands were sweaty, but my heart was steady. Suddenly, I wasn't just flying a plane; I was floating above all my troubles and worries. I felt calm. I even stopped burping.

That was when Olive grabbed for the stick. "Let's do a loop-de-loop!"

The plane lurched.

"Hold on there, missy!" yelped Mr. Selff. He regained control.

Olive flopped back against her seat. "Bah," she muttered, crossing her arms.

Mr. Selff circled back toward Rolling Hills. We found ourselves flying above Pewey Park once more.

"Okay, kids, time to write!" he shouted. "What should we say?"

"I know! I know!" shouted Olive. "How

about: 'Come to the Save the Park Protest at Pewey Park Today at Ten o'Clock. We will have posters, candy, balloon animals, a parade, mermaid swimming, and much, much more!'" She patted herself on the back. "Good, huh?"

"Not bad," shouted Mr. Selff, "but sky-writing has to be short."

"And truthful," shouted Mrs. Roosevelt.

"'Save Our Park, Rally at 10,'" I suggested . . . er . . . shouted.

"Boring!" shouted Olive. She was able to lean forward just enough to say something in Mr. Selff's ear.

He gave her a thumbs-up.

"What'd you tell him?" I shouted at her.

But before she could shout back, Mr. Selff pushed a button. Billowy white smoke started puffing from the plane's exhaust.

"Brace yourselves!" he shouted.

We dropped.

Mr. Selff banked left, forming the last letter. Then he flipped off the smoke switch. Circling, we did a fly-by so we could admire our message.

"Very nice!" shouted Mrs. Roosevelt.

We came around.

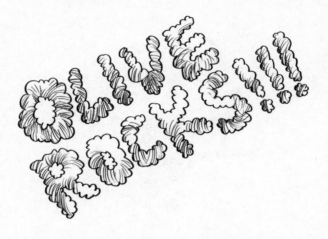

Beside me, Olive cheered.

I burped.

# CHAPTER SEVENTEEN

**TOMMY TUTTLE WAS WAITING** for us when we got home. The second I climbed out of the Buick, the sneak leaped out of our lilac bush and ran up to me.

"Amelia Earhart, HA!" He did the big *HA!* right in my face.

I stumbled backward. Hadn't I seen the kid bicycling away earlier? And why didn't he brush his teeth more often? Pee-ew, his breath stank like bacon jerky.

"What do you want, Tommy?" I asked.

"Yeah, what's all the *HA*ing about?" said Olive.

"I know who she is." He pointed to Mrs. Roosevelt. "She's Amelia Earhart."

"Wrong. HA!" retorted Olive.

"But I saw her. She was flying in an airplane."

"So?" I said. "I was flying in it too, but that doesn't make me Amelia Earhart."

"Or me," added Olive. She pointed at Mr. Selff. "Hey, maybe *he's* Amelia Earhart. . . . HA!"

Behind her, Mr. Selff cracked up. He started wheezing and guffawing and pounding his cane on the front walk.

I stared at him. Seriously. It wasn't that funny.

Mrs. Roosevelt broke in. "We do not have time for such a nonsensical conversation. May I remind you that we have less than an hour until the protest rally?" She turned to Tommy. "I am not Amelia Earhart. Now, please excuse us, we have important work to do."

"But I looked it up on Factopedia," he argued. "After I saw you in that plane, I went home and searched 'women from history who flew airplanes.' Amelia Earhart was the first hit."

Olive put her hands on her hips. "Oh, yeah?" she said. "Well, guess what, Mr. Giant Snoop Head? Factopedia is *not* a reliable source."

"What? That's not true!" argued Tommy.

"It *is* true. Anyone can edit it, which can make the entries all wrong." Olive patted herself on the back. "You'd know that if you'd gone to technology camp like me."

Tommy's cheeks turned red.

"HA!" I said right in his face.

He went limp. Seriously, it looked like somebody had let out all his air. He balled his hands into the pockets of his trench coat. A strip of bacon jerky fell to the grass, but he didn't bother to pick it up. He just slumped away. When he reached the sidewalk, though, he turned back. "I *will* uncover the truth," he declared.

"Arrr-woof!" replied Fala. He gobbled down the dropped piece of jerky.

\* \* \*

An hour later, we pulled Olive's wagon— piled high with signs and posters—into Pewey Park. Mr. Selff was driving and had offered to take us, but honestly, it was a lot faster to walk.

It was a pretty nice morning. Yellow dandelions freckled the thick green grass, and a soft breeze rustled through the branches of the big shade trees. Bees buzzed in the flowers. Butterflies flitted around. And Fala joyfully lifted his leg on Mr. Pewey's bronze boots. I shook my head in disbelief. In just a few hours, all this could be gone.

*Buh-dop!* It was my phone again.

I looked over at the bulldozers.

Chuck waved.

Buzz bared his teeth.

I tapped out a lie . . . I mean, reply.

Mrs. Roosevelt was taping posters to tree trunks. Olive and I helped by piling up all the picket signs we'd made the night before. Obviously, Mrs. Roosevelt had stayed up and made more . . . *lots* more.

"Why so many?" asked Olive.

"I expect a crowd after all our communication efforts," replied the First Lady. "And I am positive they will want to join in our protest."

I sure hoped so.

Mrs. Roosevelt strode briskly around, checking up on our work. Finally, she said, "It is time."

"But nobody's here," I said.

"Not yet," replied Mrs. Roosevelt. "But I have great faith in the good sense of the citizenry."

She picked up a sign, raised it high, and began marching back and forth in front of the statue. "Save Pewey Park!" she chanted. "Save Pewey Park!"

Olive congaed along behind her. "Pewey-Pewey-Pew-*ee*! Pewey-Pewey-Pew-*ee*!"

Even Fala got in the act. He frisked after them wearing a little sign that read "Whatever is asked of us, I am sure we can accomplish it."

Mrs. Roosevelt had obviously made *that* after we went to bed too. Geez, did the woman ever rest? And how did she come up with such lame poster slogans? There wasn't a single exclamation point on any of them!!!

That was when Mr. Selff finally arrived. "You wouldn't believe the traffic on Keystone Street," he said. "A motorcyclist *and* a jogger."

He hobbled over to the pile of protest signs and plucked one out.

Olive had made it.

"Pretty good likeness," said Mr. Selff. He got in line behind Fala. "Save Pewey Park! Save Pewey Park!"

"Come on, Nolan," called Olive.

"Raise your voice!" declared Mrs. Roosevelt.

"What are you waiting for, son?" asked Mr. Selff.

*For a giant bald eagle to swoop down and carry me away,* I thought. What was the point of marching around all by ourselves? Still, I reluctantly grabbed a sign and followed along.

"Save Pewey Park!"

"Pewey-Pewey-Pew-*ee*!"

*"Arrr-woof!"*

Oh, brother.

We marched back and forth.

Up and down.

Around and around.

On the other side of the baseball diamond, Chuck and Buzz watched us. They

laughed so hard they had to pound each other on the back.

It was pretty humiliating.

Just then a group of little kids wearing bright yellow T-shirts and name tags shaped like bulldozers shuffled into the park. I groaned. Oh, geez, not the Pitter-Patter day campers.

Their counselor, Miss Missy, clapped her

hands. "Look over there, boys and girls. Do you see what I see? Bulldozers!"

A boy named Paulie stuck out his lower lip. "I don't like bulldozers. I like digger trucks."

"Me too," said a boy named Braydon.

"I like roller trucks," said a girl named Ava.

"Me too," said Braydon.

"Dump trucks!"

"Cement trucks!"

"I like corn!" cried a kid named Clarence. "I eat corn every night."

"Me too," said Braydon.

Miss Missy blew a strand of hair out of her sweaty face and started arranging the kids on the grass. "Crisscross applesauce," she said. "Pretzel legs. On your gumdrops."

"I'm hungry!" cried Paulie.

"Me too!" cried Braydon.

Olive elbowed me in the ribs. "Told you we should have handed out candy."

"We'll have snacks later, boys and girls," chirped Miss Missy. "But now we're going to watch the bulldozers do their work. Won't that be fun?"

"It'd be funner if it was digger trucks," grumbled Paulie.

"Or corn," added Clarence.

The park was really starting to fill with people now. It seemed like practically everyone in town was there. I scanned the crowd and saw Mr. Treble and Mrs. Bustamante and Mr. Jolly. Alden Wurlitzer was there in his new high-tops. He waggled his fingers at Olive. She waggled back. And there was Alex in a clean White Sox shirt and C. J. McCabe and the shoe-store sales guy and—of all the rotten luck!—Heather Lynne. I pretended not to see her.

Mr. Selff puffed out his chest. "Guess my skywriting did the trick."

"That and my Kidschat post," said Olive.

"It was the mystic chords of democracy," Mrs. Roosevelt corrected them. She turned to me. "Nolan, help me hand out the picket signs to our fellow protestors, won't you?"

I swear she practically skipped over to the pile. Her eyes were glowing brighter than Olive's new shoes, and her smile was so big it showed her crooked teeth.

"Good moooorning, Rolling Hills!"

Mayor Selff, wearing a gold construction hat and carrying a matching gold shovel, bounded past Mrs. Roosevelt and the protest signs. She took the band shell's stairs in a single leap.

"Are you ready to break new ground?" she cried.

The crowd cheered.

"I'm sure that, like me, many of you thought this day would never come," continued the mayor. "But here we are at last, embracing progress and transforming Pewey Park into . . ." She paused dramatically. "The Selff parking lot!"

The crowd cheered again.

And Mrs. Roosevelt dropped the sign she'd been holding. "It seems I have made a mistake. None of these people have come to protest. None are here to save the park."

"It doesn't look that way," I said. I felt awful—for me, for the park, but most of all for Mrs. Roosevelt. I mean, she really believed all that stuff about speaking up and making a difference. It must have hurt that it wasn't working.

"Nobody came to our protest!" wailed Olive.

"I guess you really can't beat city hall," I said.

Mrs. Roosevelt shook her head sternly. "I will not believe that."

I didn't want to believe it either. But it was hard to ignore the truth when pretty much the whole town was over by the band shell shouting "Progress! Progress! Progress!" Geez, even Fala had joined the crowd, but that was mostly because the day campers were gnawing on dino-grahams and the dog was giving them the Treatment.

The mayor stepped back onto the grass. She lowered her shovel. "One the count of three," she cried. "One . . . two . . ."

"Three!" shouted the crowed.

The mayor dug deep into the dirt.

At the same moment, the bulldozers started up.

Mayor Selff held her shovelful of dirt high so everyone could see it.

And so the photographer from our local newspaper the *Rolling Hills Doings* could snap her picture.

The bulldozers growled. Waiting. Eager.

My heart started to pound. Any second now, the mayor would give the signal and the big trucks would move across the lawn, destroying everything in their path.

It couldn't happen.

Somebody had to do something.

It wasn't right. It wasn't fair.

"Stop!" a voice shouted. "Put down that shovel!"

"Who is that?" cried the mayor. "Who's shouting?"

I looked around.

Olive was staring at me openmouthed.

So was Mr. Selff.

Even Fala looked up from the sticky fingers he was licking.

Only Mrs. Roosevelt was nodding and smiling.

And that was when it hit me.

The person shouting . . . was *me*!

## CHAPTER EIGHTEEN

**I DON'T KNOW WHERE** courage comes from, exactly. The only thing I really know for sure is that when the bulldozers started up, I knew I had to stop them. I shoved my way through the crowd and took a giant step right into the mayor. Then I stood on my tiptoes until our noses were almost touching and I said, "Stop this . . . *now!*"

Mayor Selff backed up. She made herself smile. "I'm afraid it's too late."

"But I don't want a Selff parking lot,"

I said. "I want a park. Pewey Park. A place to play and rest and—"

"Skateboard!" called Olive.

"I can't reverse the decision," said the mayor.

A colony of flapping bats formed in my stomach. "Yes you can. You're the mayor. You can do anything you want."

The mayor shrugged. "My hands are tied. As the town's elected official, I am simply acting on the citizens' will. Obviously, they

approve of this project. Just look at the enthusiastic turnout." She patted me on the
shoulder. "Why don't you go join your grand-
mother over there and be quiet."

*Be quiet?*

I stood there, frozen. What was happening to me? What did I think I was doing?
Then it occurred to me: Maybe this was one
of those "moments of truth" that happen to a
person sometimes. You know, one of those
all-important times in your life when you
have to decide what you're really made of.
Whether you're going to follow through with
something you believe in or make it easy on
yourself, turn around, and run the other way.

Behind us the bulldozers revved.

I took a deep breath and turned to the
crowd. "Some ... um, *many* ... of my best
memories belong to this park. Or, er, belong
to me *in* this park," I stammered. "When I
was little, my mom and dad would bring me

here all the time. My mom played catch with me, and my dad pushed me on the swings."

I felt a weird catch in my throat. I wished my dad were here now, rooting me on.

"Hey, what about me?" cried Olive.

"Those were the days before my sister was born," I added. I smiled. "Good times."

"Humph," snorted Olive.

I went on. "I bet lots of you have had good times here too. Like you, Mr. Treble." I pointed at him. "Remember all those concerts your accordion group gave in the band shell? You sure looked like you were having fun."

Mr. Treble nodded.

"And you, Mr. Jolly. Weren't some of your prizewinning roses growing up the park's trellis? Just over there. You donated them, right?"

"They were Golden Celebrations, in honor of my wedding anniversary," he said.

I scanned the crowd. "How many of you played in the state bocce ball tournament the day Rolling Hills become the Illinois champs? What a great day that was, huh? And it happened right over there." I gave a nervous laugh. "And I bet practically everybody here has picnicked or played Frisbee on this lawn. I bet some of you have even sat and read a book in the shade of the big trees." My eyes found Mrs. Bustamante. "I know *you* have."

The corners of the librarian's mouth turned up.

"So why do we want to lose all this? Sure, parking lots are convenient and all, but Pewey Park is . . . well . . ." I cast around for the words to express how I felt. "It's . . . it's the heart of our town."

After that, I went quiet, like everything I'd been thinking and feeling had tumbled out and I had nothing more to say. My arms dropped to my sides and I let out this big sigh. Suddenly, I felt awkward. Everyone was just standing there looking at one another. Even the day campers had gotten quiet.

Then Mr. Treble turned his eyes away from me and walked stiffly off.

Mr. Jolly stared at his shoes. He untied them, tied them, and untied them again. After a second, he walked away too, laces flapping.

So did Mrs. Bustamante, and Mrs. Cordero, who I knew for a fact was captain of the bocce ball team the year it won the championship.

Lots of other people just turned and walked away too.

I don't know what I'd been expecting. But it wasn't that. I sat down on the grass and pulled my knees up to hide my face.

The bulldozers growled.

Olive came over and tapped me on the shoulder. "You okay?"

I pushed her hand away. "Fine."

There was a pause. "It's not your fault no one came to our protest. You were awesome sauce, Nolan, with sprinkles on top. Wasn't he, Ellie?"

"Mrs. Roosevelt," insisted Mrs. Roosevelt. "And you were very courageous, Nolan."

"I'm proud of you, son," added Mr. Selff.

I got to my feet. Officer Nittles was directing people to a safe area marked off with yellow caution tape. We joined the crowd, but I didn't have the heart to stick around and watch. "Let's go," I said. "It's over. We lost."

Suddenly, a loud grinding noise came from the bulldozers. Black smoke puffed from their exhaust pipes. Side by side they crept forward, their blades churning up everything in front of them. From where I stood, I could see Chuck clutching the big steering wheel and grinning ear to ear. In the next truck, Buzz drew back his lips to show his teeth. He reminded me of a wolf. A hungry wolf.

The crowd groaned as the bulldozers ripped! Slashed! Gashed!

"I hate bulldozers!" cried Paulie, scrunching up his face.

"Me too!" cried Braydon. The boys grabbed each other's hands.

"I have had quite enough of this," said Mrs. Roosevelt. Without a backward glance, she ducked under the yellow tape and strode briskly toward the bulldozers.

"Halt!" she ordered, holding up her hand.

The bulldozers rolled to a stop.

Chuck poked his head out the window. "Hey, lady, move it!"

Buzz poked his head out his window too. "Did you find your pooch?"

That was when Mrs. Roosevelt did this crazy thing:

Beside me, Mr. Selff whistled admiringly. "That woman never quits."

Beside him, Olive boxed the air. "Atta girl, Ellie! You show 'em!"

"I like Ellie," said Paulie.

"Me too," said Braydon.

"No, no, no!" shrieked the mayor. She

wheeled on Officer Nittles. "Arrest that woman!"

The policewoman shook her head. "There's no law against lying down in a public park."

"The mayor's face turned so red it was almost purple, like a grape, or an eggplant. "Arrest her for being a menace to public safety, then."

Officer Nittles shook her head again. "I don't see how her lying out there poses any threat to the folks standing back here."

Mayor Selff squinted at the policewoman. "I don't think you want to help me, Florence."

Officer Nittles shrugged.

And the mayor screamed. I'm not kidding. She balled her fists and stamped her feet and screamed long and loud. *"Arggggggggggggggh!"*

Then she stormed over to Mrs. Roosevelt. "Get up! You're ruining everything. You're blocking progress." She grabbed the

First Lady's arm and tried to drag her out of the bulldozers' way. "Get uuuuup!"

Mrs. Roosevelt said, "No."

Mayor Selff let go of Mrs. Roosevelt's arm. She stood over her, panting, trying to get herself back under control. "Why?" she finally said. "It's just a park. Why do you care so much?"

"Because somebody has to," I replied.

The mayor whirled. She hadn't seen me coming across the grass. Ignoring her furious expression, I lay down next to Mrs. Roosevelt.

"Nothing has ever been achieved by the person who says 'It can't be done,'" I said.

"Well put, Nolan," said Mrs. Roosevelt. "May I quote you in my future?"

"I'll look for it in the history books," I said.

Olive came squealing across the grass. "I care too!" She lay down next to me.

"So do I," said Mr. Selff.

It was a struggle, what with his bad knees and all, but he managed to get down next to Olive.

Even Fala joined us. He lay down on the other side of Mrs. Roosevelt.

"Daaad, get up," whined the mayor. "Everybody's staring. You're embarrassing me."

"Tough taters," retorted Mr. Selff.

That was when we heard . . .

"*Oom-pa-pa! Oom-pa-pa!*"

Mr. Selff raised his head. "That sounds like . . ."

"An accordion," said Mrs. Roosevelt.

We all raised our heads.

It *was* an accordion. Seven of them, actually. Led by Mr. Treble, the accordion group marched across the grass and into the band shell.

"We're taking requests, folks," Mr. Treble called out.

Officer Nittles cupped her mouth. "Can you play 'Far, Far Away'?"

It took people a couple seconds to get the double meaning. Then they laughed. I guess accordion music isn't all that popular. Still, the crowd pushed through the yellow tape to mingle and talk and polka on the lawn. Officer Nittles didn't try to stop them.

Mrs. Cordero came back too. She'd changed into her state bocce champs T-shirt. So had about twelve other people with her. I figured they were her teammates. The matching medals hanging around their necks were kind of a giveaway. In seconds, they'd set up the bocce court and started inviting people to play.

Others spread out blankets and popped open lawn furniture. Frisbees whizzed through the air. Kites took flight. Pretty soon there were tables heaped with all sorts of food—watermelon, hot dogs, potato salad . . .

"Meatballs!" whooped Olive.

*"Arrrf!"* In a flash, Fala was up and begging.

Mr. Jolly actually smiled at the dog as he

set a big vase of fresh-cut roses in the middle of it all. It was practically a holiday or something.

"I like picnics," said Paulie.

"Me too," said Braydon.

"I guess the citizens have spoken," I said to the mayor.

"So they have." She sighed. "Still, I would have liked having a parking lot named after me."

She signaled for the bulldozers to leave.

Buzz growled almost as loudly as the dozers before they rumbled away.

"Good riddance," said Mrs. Roosevelt.

"Drive safely!" called Mr. Selff.

"Darlene!" It was Mrs. Bustamante. She ran up and grabbed the mayor's hands. "It's marvelous, this whole party-in-the-park thing. Rolling Hills should do it every year. Why, it's absolutely the most perfect way to bring the community together. We could call it the Selff Annual Picnic. What do you think?"

The mayor beamed. "I think you're brilliant, Monica."

They walked away arm in arm.

It was time for us to go too. "The radio is sure to turn on any second now," I said. "I think we've learned what we needed to learn from you."

"Oh, I do hope so," said Mrs. Roosevelt. "Now that my work is done *here,* I am eager to return to my work *there.*"

"No rest for the weary?" said Mr. Selff.

She blinked. "Who is weary?"

We all got to our feet, and Mrs. Roosevelt called for Fala. Then we headed out of the park.

"Hey, Nolan, hold up!"

I turned.

It was Heather Lynne. She smiled. "I just wanted to say, what you did back there? It was amazing."

I tried to smile back, but my mouth was suddenly so dry my lips got stuck on my gums. I probably looked like I was making faces at her. "Heh, heh," I said. I sounded like a real idiot.

"So I'll be seeing you later today?"

"Heh, heh . . . later?"

"At the big game against Fred and Ethel's Cleaning Service, remember?"

"Oh, heh, heh, right."

"See you there," she said.

I watched her walk away. "Heh, heh, not if I see you first," I muttered to myself.

# CHAPTER NINETEEN

**"I DON'T GET IT,"** I said.

We were standing around the crystal radio once more. Five minutes earlier, I'd pulled it out of the kitchen cabinet, where I'd shoved it earlier before heading to the park, and set it on the counter. Then I'd braced myself for white light, blurry vision, bubbles. Instead . . .

"Nothing," said Olive.

"I don't get it," I said again. I could feel my frustration building, the bats flapping away in my stomach. "We learned, right?

We learned from the past how to live in the present."

Mr. Selff leaned in for a closer look. We'd told him all about the crystal radio on the *slooow* drive back from the park. Believe it or not, he hadn't acted doubtful or astonished. He'd just nodded and called me Horatio again.

Really, who *was* that guy?

Mrs. Roosevelt touched the radio's headphones. "Could there be a mechanical malfunction, Nolan?"

I didn't think so. Still, I checked the dials and connectors. Everything looked to be in working order.

"I don't get it," I said for the third time.

Olive said, "Maybe H.H. wants Ellie to stick around for a while."

H.H.! The bats in my belly started flapping even harder, and angry words started to pile up. Boy, was I going to give H.H. a piece of my mind if I ever met him. That is, if H.H. wasn't an ax murderer or a zombie or something.

I looked over at Mrs. Roosevelt. I could tell she was upset too. Not only had she let Olive get away with calling her Ellie, but she'd started rocking back and forth again.

"Mrs. Roosevelt?" I said.

She rocked.

"Eleanor?" said Mr. Selff.

She rocked some more.

"Snap out of it!" bellowed Olive.

Mrs. Roosevelt jerked and shook herself. A second later she said, "Thank you, Olive. Self-pity is such an unrewarding indulgence."

"No prob, Ellie," said Olive.

"It is Mrs. Roosevelt," corrected Mrs. Roosevelt.

Mr. Selff and I grinned at each other. The First Lady was back.

Mrs. Roosevelt swiped her hands together briskly. "It seems to me that while we wait for the radio, we should put our time to good use. Are there any other tasks we can accomplish? Any wrongs to make right? We make a fine team."

Definitely back.

"You know what would be a good use of time?" suggested Olive. "TV."

Mr. Selff nodded his agreement.

"Or ice cream," added Olive.

"*Aaarf!*" barked Fala.

"I meant," said the First Lady, "that we should use our time doing consequential things, not puff stuff."

Olive wrinkled her nose. "But all work and no play is no fun."

"Work time *is* my play time."

Olive turned to me, her expression pleading: "*You* play with her for a while, okay, Nolan?"

"I believe Nolan has a sporting event to attend," said Mrs. Roosevelt.

Oh, right. She'd been there for the conversation with Heather—if you could count me going "heh, heh" as a part of a conversation.

I let out a big, dramatic sigh. Wasn't flying an airplane and giving a speech and lying down in front of bulldozers enough for one day? Did I have to go kick a ball around too?

"I'm not going," I said.

"But you made a commitment," said Mrs. Roosevelt.

"The team doesn't need me," I replied. "Not now. Not with Heather Lynne on it."

Mrs. Roosevelt watched me for a long moment. "No one can make you feel inferior without your consent," she finally said.

"Huh?" said Olive.

"Allow me to tell you a story," said Mrs. Roosevelt.

That is my mother, Anna Hall Roosevelt. Is she not beautiful? She was the belle of the ball in New York society.

Other people called me worse.

So mortified was I by my physical appearance that I began spending all of my time at home. Alone.

Oh, how I wished to be pretty!

Then, one Thanksgiving morning, my father took me for a carriage ride.

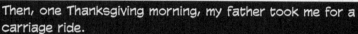

Where are we going?

To the Newsboys' Lodging House, missy. It's a place for homeless boys who make their living selling newspapers.

But why are we going?

You shall see.

I had barely set foot in the place before a ladle was pressed into my hand.

Start scooping.

Pinch-faced boys, some no older than myself, held out their plates for potatoes. The boys were thin. Ragged. All alone in the world.

At first, I felt too insecure to look them in the eye. Surely the boys would make fun of my appearance. But . . .

This is the best meal I've had in weeks.

I liked that feeling.

Later, I pondered the day. I had convinced myself that I was worthless because I was not pretty. But now I thought . . .

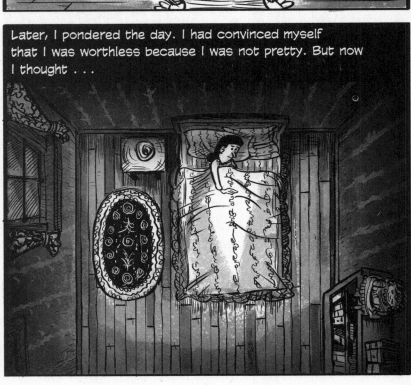

... so what if people made fun of my looks? I did not have to listen to them. I did not have to believe them. I would not allow myself to feel inferior.

I would be truthful, loyal, and brave. I would try to make lasting changes in people's lives.

What could be more beautiful than that?

What could a guy do after a story like that?

I went up to my room and put on my soccer uniform.

When I came back down, Mrs. Roosevelt was waiting to go with me.

I tried to talk her out of it. "Someone might recognize you," I argued. "Or, hey, what if the radio comes back on?"

I wasn't really worried about either of those things happening. I just didn't want to be humiliated in front of my teammates, their parents, *and* the First Lady of the United States.

"It is my duty to provide moral support," Mrs. Roosevelt said firmly.

"But it's a game," I tried again. "A waste of time. Puff stuff."

She held up a notepad and pencil. "I shall dash off my daily newspaper column while you are playing—four hundred chatty words about the small happenings in my life. After all, travel to the future is no excuse for shirking one's commitment to one's readers."

Oh, brother!

At least Olive wouldn't be there. Mr. Selff had volunteered to "occupy the little miss."

"Let's watch *Mermaid Adventures* and then have a tea party. We can wear tiaras. Fala too," bossed Olive.

Poor Mr. Selff! As Mrs. Roosevelt and I left the house, we could hear her shouting out orders.

* * *

By the time we got to the soccer field, my team was already out there, chipping and passing and warming up. Heather Lynne juggled a ball from foot to foot and from thigh to thigh. She bounced it off the top of her head.

My shoulders drooped.

"Confidence," Mrs. Roosevelt whispered

in my ear. She took a seat in the bleachers and opened her notepad. Touching the tip of her pencil to her tongue, she thought for a second, then started writing.

"Hey, Stanberry, where in the heck have you been?" shouted Coach Filbert. "I thought we were going to have to play without a forward. Take your position. Hustle!"

I trotted out to the field.

"All right, Nolan," hollered my coach again. "I'm going to kick a couple your way. Get ready!"

Heather and some of the other players turned to watch, and Coach tapped me a ground ball.

I was nervous as anything. I could actually feel all those eyes—Heather's, my other teammates', the crowd's, even Mrs. Roosevelt's—everyone watching and waiting for me to mess up.

I kept my eyes on the ball as it left the

coach's foot, followed it as it rolled toward me, saw it bump against my cleat. I just stood still. I broke out in a cold sweat.

"Whaddya doin' out there, Stanberry?" called Coach Filbert. "I've seen zombies kick harder."

My shoulders drooped even lower than before.

"Let's try this again," Coach shouted. "And this time, look alive!"

I glanced over at Mrs. Roosevelt. She laid her notepad aside and mouthed, "Confidence."

I tried to fake it. I tried to act cool and self-assured. But it didn't work. When I attempted to knock the dirt off my cleats, I ended up accidentally kicking myself in my shin guard.

C.J. snickered.

Coach Filbert tapped another ball to me. I concentrated on it.

"Confidence," I whispered to myself. "Confidence."

*Schwap!*

I kicked it back. No spinning. Straight on the nose and not too hard. It was a pretty decent one. A good pass.

In the bleachers, Mrs. Roosevelt clapped. She even peeled off her gloves so it sounded louder. "Bravo, Nolan! Well done!"

My nerves settled a little.

"Okay, Stanberry, here comes another one."

This time it was an air ball. As soon as I saw it coming, I ran toward it and trapped it with my chest. Then I let it drop and chipped it over to C.J.

My shoulders relaxed. Not bad. So what if I wasn't Heather "Superstar" Lynne? That didn't mean my soccer skills were complete baby drool. I still knew how to pass and chip and trap. I could still be useful to the team.

I looked up at Mrs. Roosevelt. She was on the edge of her bleacher seat now, her high-beam gaze focused on me. I waved. She waved back.

A few minutes later, the referee blew her whistle and the game began.

Twenty kids raced up and down the field, dribbling and passing, huffing and puffing.

In the bleachers, parents cheered.

"Go, Heather, go!"

And—

"Kick that ball, C.J.!"

And—

"Way to play, Denzel!"

And—

"Try your very utmost, Pests!" The voice was fluttery and high-pitched, even more so when it added, "Whoooo!"

No way! I whirled just as the ref blew for the two-minute break. And my jaw dropped practically to my knees. Mrs. Roosevelt was . . .

Cheerleading! Hand-clapping, foot-hopping, chant-shouting cheerleading.

"Give me a *T*!" she shouted.

"*T!*" the crowd shouted back.

"Give me an *R*!"

"*R!*"

"Give me a *Y*!"

"*Y!*"

"What does that spell?" cried Mrs. Roosevelt.

The parents looked at each other, lips moving, confused.

"Uh . . . er . . . *try?*" Mr. McCabe finally ventured.

He must have gotten it right, because Mrs. Roosevelt started hopping up and down so wildly that her hairnet slipped sideways. She shouted, "The only failure is in not trying. Whoooo!"

I shook my head. What had gotten into her? She was acting *very* un-First-Lady-like. It was like some alien had sucked out her personality and replaced it with one belonging to a Dallas Cowboys cheerleader.

Only Mrs. Roosevelt's cheerleading kinda stank.

"Win as a team. That is the way! A team must have moxie, be skillful and smart. A team is the sum of its separate parts! Whoooo!"

Moxie?

"Hey, Stanberry," called C.J. "Your grandma is . . ." He made the cuckoo sign.

Heather shot back, "Her cheers are awesome, McCabe. You should be . . ." She gave him the "for shame" sign, rubbing her pointer finger over her other pointer finger.

C.J. fired back with a rude gesture that I'm not allowed to describe.

"Persist, persist, and on to victory. To think in any other way is contradictory!" cheered Mrs. Roosevelt.

Oh, brother!

The ref blasted her whistle again.

The Pests played hard. In the last quarter,

I even beat four kids on the dribble to hoof the ball straight to the goal. Then I fired off a cannonball.

*Thwunk!*

It glanced off the crossbar of the goalpost and on the rebound whacked Coach Filbert right in the face.

My face burned ... maybe even more than Coach's.

"Good try!" shouted Heather.

"Give your best and you will prevail. To never try assures you will fail! Whoooo!" cheered Mrs. Roosevelt.

*That's actually true,* I thought. *It* is. *Whoooo!*

In the end, Fred and Ethel's Cleaning Service mopped us up. But not before Mrs. Roosevelt got everyone in the bleachers to shout, "Give your all—that is all we need. In this way, we all succeed!"

Afterward, parents gathered around her

to compliment her on her "team spirit" and "sense of fun." Honest, they called her "fun."

She smiled a huge smile that showed bad teeth and real joy. "It *was* amusing, was it not?" She sounded almost surprised.

At some point during the game, she'd pulled off her hairnet, freeing her once–tightly wound curls. Now a few strands of hair blew across her face. She laughed and tucked them behind her ear, then held up a juice box someone had given her.

"Have you ever had one of these, Nolan? They are delicious *and* entertaining. Watch!" Squeezing the box, she caught the stream of juice that spouted from its straw in her open, waiting mouth. She swallowed. "You know, I don't remember when I have had such an enjoyable time. Perhaps I should start a White House soccer league. The Supreme Court would make nine excellent cheerleaders. I imagine we could set up on the South Lawn."

*Buh-dop*, went my phone.

An hour?

"Oh, geez, Mrs. Roosevelt," I said. "We need to—"

Beaming, she interrupted, "Call me Eleanor."

"Eleanor." Her name felt weird on my tongue. I tried again. "Eleanor, we need to—"

*Honk! Honk! Honk! Honk!*

Mr. Selff's gold Buick crawled over to the curb. Olive and Fala poked their heads out the back window.

"Hurry and get in!" cried Olive. "It's on! The radio—it turned itself on!"

She didn't have to tell us twice. Mrs. Roosevelt—er, Eleanor and I bolted for the car.

I was just getting into the backseat when Heather called out to me. "See you tomorrow at practice?"

I turned. Straightened. Smiled. "Yeah, sure. I—"

Olive grabbed the back of my uniform and tugged. "Get in, already."

I fell back onto the seat, and Olive slammed the door.

"Buckle up," said Mr. Selff. He was still wearing a mermaid Princess Aquamarina tiara from the tea party. Putting on his turn signal, he checked his side mirror five times before creeping away from the curb. We inched down the street.

"Put the pedal to the medal!" hollered Olive.

*"Aaarf!"* barked Fala.

Behind us a blue minivan honked impatiently. At the first opportunity, it veered around us.

All my muscles clenched. How long would the radio stay on?

"Please, Mr. Selff, speed up," I urged.

"Yes, perhaps a tad faster, Howard," said Eleanor.

"I'm going as fast as I dare," he replied. But he pressed the accelerator. The car went from inching to crawling.

"Hurry!" said Olive.

"Yes, do hurry," said Eleanor.

*"Aaaarf!"* barked Fala.

After what seemed like about ten years, Mr. Selff made a wide, slow turn into our driveway. The car rolled to a stop and we leaped out.

"Go! Go!" cried Mr. Selff. He fumbled with the keys, the door, his cane. "Don't wait for this old heap."

We sprinted around the corner to the front door . . .

And came to a screeching halt.

Tommy Tuttle was sitting cross-legged on the front stoop, nonchalantly chomping on a strip of bacon jerky.

# CHAPTER TWENTY

**"OH, COME ON!" CRIED** Olive. "You, *again?*"

"What can I say?" replied Tommy with a shrug. "A good detective is persistent." He

stood and tucked the unfinished strip of jerky into a pocket of his trench coat.

Fala raised his nose and sniffed the air.

"Some unusual things have been going on in your house, Stanberry," Tommy said with a greasy smirk.

Behind him, the radio's white light blinked out from between the cracks of the window blinds.

I felt tingly with panic. How much longer would the radio stay on? Any second now, it could go dark, leaving Eleanor trapped in the twenty-first century.

"Move it!" I growled.

"Or I'll turn on my shoes!" added Olive.

Eleanor laid a hand on my sister's shoulder. "Stay calm, dear."

Fala trotted forward and, rearing up on his hind legs, sniff-sniff-sniffed Tommy's pocket.

Tommy pushed him away. "This has been a tough case to crack, but I always get my man. I mean, woman." He shook his head. "Whatever! I finally put two and two together, and it equals—"

"Four," interrupted Olive. She looked around at us. "Duh!"

"No, it equals the truth." Tommy put his hand on his chin and rubbed imaginary whiskers. "Allow me to elucidate."

"Huh?" said Olive.

"It's the detective word for *explain*," I told her. I knew that from the Mysterious Mysteries graphic novel series.

Fala began tugging on the hem of Tommy's trench coat.

Tommy was too busy elucidating to notice. "As I was saying . . . clue number one: she is not Amelia Earhart. Clue number two: she has a little dog. Clue number three: she has a funny-sounding voice."

"I beg your pardon," said Eleanor stiffly.

"Clue number four . . ." Tommy paused.

In the quiet, I could faintly hear static coming from the radio.

That was when Mr. Selff shuffled up behind us. He took in the situation in a flash. "Move aside, young man," he said to Tommy.

"I don't take orders from old guys in crowns," Tommy replied.

"It's a tiara, not a crown," said Olive. "Consider yourself elucidated."

The static had gotten louder, and was it my imagination, or was the world starting to go blurry? I recognized those signs. Eleanor had to go *now*.

"Tiara. Crown. Who cares?" Tommy was saying. "It's all stupid mermaid stuff."

Olive put her hands on her hips. "Repeat that. I dare you!"

With a smirk, Tommy said it again: "Stupid mermaid stuff."

"You asked for it!" said Olive. She let him have it . . . with her shoes.

"Wowza!" shouted Tommy. He squeezed his eyes shut and stumbled backward.

At the same time, Fala lunged. Leaping into the air, he grabbed the end of the trench coat's belt and tugged.

Dog and boy twirled. From the coat's many pockets flew a magnifying glass, a note-pad, a pencil, a vial of something green, a Sherlock Holmes action figure, a pair of mini binoculars, and three strips of bacon jerky.

Tommy lunged for his detective equipment.

Fala lunged for the jerky.

The two met in midair, bouncing off each other like bowling pins and rolling down the two steps to the walkway.

That was when Tommy realized that his coat was open—and that we could all see what he was wearing underneath it.

"Hector the Hedgehog underpants!" exclaimed Olive. "Va-va-va-voom!"

Tommy clutched the coat around him.

"I . . . I can explain," he stammered. "I was in the middle of trying on the new underwear my mom bought for me when I put two and two together, and . . ."

We didn't wait to hear the rest. In a flash, we were through the door and headed into the kitchen.

A second later, Mr. Selff caught up with us. "I locked the door," he said.

He joined us in front of the radio.

The pop and crackle from the headphones were louder now. Then the noise seemed to form words. Through the static I clearly heard the word "home."

"It's time!" I said.

Eleanor nodded. "Fala, come!" she called.

Obediently, the Scottish terrier snatched his rubber bone off the rug and leaped into her arms.

I turned to Olive. "It's up to you. You have to do it exactly the way you did it earlier. You know, when you brought Fala here. Got it?"

"Got it," said Olive. She put on the headphones and reached for the dial.

"Wait!" cried Eleanor. "I cannot leave without saying goodbye."

She hurried over to Mr. Selff and took his hands in hers. "I shall be looking for you in my future."

"You think you'll recognize me without all these wrinkles?" he asked.

She smiled. "You, Howard, are unforgettable."

The static in the headphones grew louder and more insistent.

Eleanor turned to Olive. "And you, dear girl. Do not ever lose your spirit. It will serve you well." She leaned over and kissed Olive's right cheek.

Fala licked her left one.

"Time to go," I urged.

In the whirl of sound, the word "home" was being repeated over and over.

Eleanor turned to me. "You learn by living," she said. "We *both* discovered that today, Nolan." She winked. "Because of you, I am going to let my hair down more often in the future. Well, in *my* future."

"Enough, already!" hollered Olive. "The sound is fading!"

Eleanor stepped back and clutched Fala to her chest.

Olive reached for the dial. "Good-bye, Ellie!"

"Good-bye, Ollie!" she called back, her voice already garbled and sputtering with static.

*Click . . . click . . . click.*

The world dissolved, the room once again melting into a blur. Then—

*POP!*

The room snapped back like a rubber band and returned to focus.

Eleanor and Fala were gone.

None of us said anything right away. We just stared at the empty space where they'd been.

Finally, Mr. Selff said, "Phew! I've seen some things in my time, but that was one wild ride."

"I hope she made it back okay," said Olive.

"Oh, she made it just fine." Mr. Selff's face beamed as he reached into his wallet and pulled out a black-and-white snapshot. It was faded and creased in places. But when he handed it to me, I could still make out the picture.

"I've always wondered why she hugged me as if I were a long-lost friend," said Mr. Selff. "Now I know."

Olive peered at the photo. "I'm glad she gave up the hairnets."

"She gave those up today at the soccer game," I said.

Mr. Selff pointed at the place Eleanor had been standing. "Looks like she left you a memento."

"That's all she left?" Olive said, pouting. "A nasty old hairnet?" She turned to Mr. Selff. "Ben Franklin left us a whole electrostatic machine."

Mr. Selff's bushy eyebrows shot up. But before I could explain, the front door opened and Mom called, "Kids?"

"Mommy!" squealed Olive. She raced into the hallway to give our mother a hug.

Mr. Selff and I followed.

"Where's Eleanor?" asked Mom when she saw us. "And why did I see Tommy running down the street in his underwear? Is everything all right?"

"Allow me to elucidate," began Olive.

I cut her off. "Eleanor had to . . . um . . . leave unexpectedly," I said. "But don't worry. Mr. Selff is here."

"I don't understand. Why is—"

I changed the subject. "How was your plane ride?"

"It was good, Nolan, but I really want to hear about—"

"And the rest of your trip? Anything exciting happen?"

"Exciting? Well, it's Manhattan, so it's always exciting, honey. Now tell me what's been happening here. What did you think of Eleanor? Did you like her? Was she nice? And where in the world did Olive get those shoes?"

The last thing I wanted to talk about was Eleanor . . . or Olive's stupid shoes.

"How is your *editor*, Mom?"

If there's one subject my mother loves to blab about, it's her editor.

"Oh, Ann!" Mom slapped a hand over her heart. "She's genius, as always. I tell you, Nolan, nothing primes the creative pump like spending time with her. In fact, we already have an idea for our next book. It just sort of popped into my mind while I was in her office, and she went for it. Guess who the Bumble Bunnies are blasting back to meet next?"

I shook my head.

"Eleanor Roosevelt!" exclaimed Mom.

"Nobody will know who she is," said Olive.

Mom frowned.

·"Just saying," added Olive.

"Well, I intend to change that," said Mom. "Listen, you guys, I want to run upstairs and make a few quick notes while the idea is still fresh. Then I'll take you out for pizza. Is it a deal?"

"Deal," I said.

Mom hurried up the stairs. But at her studio doorway, she stopped. "Of course, that includes you too, Mr. Selff."

"That's very kind," said Mr. Selff. "But are you sure you want an old man like me around?"

"Are you kidding?" I said. "No one looks as good in a tiara as you do."

Mr. Selff reached up and touched his head. "Good heavens, I forgot I still had it on."

That was when Olive started doing the conga. "Pizza-pizza-pizz-AH! Pizza-pizza-pizz-AH!"

"I do like sausage," said Mr. Selff

"Sausage-sausage-sau-SAGE!" sang Olive.

Mr. Selff joined in, knees creaking, cane thumping. "Sausage-sausage-sau-SAGE!"

At the top of the stairs, Mom laughed.

And that was when it struck me. Eleanor Roosevelt hadn't just left us a hairnet. She'd left us a friend.

And *that* was something to conga about.

**THE DOORBELL RANG WHILE** I was doing my social studies homework at the kitchen table, reading about the Puritans for a report I had to turn in on Monday. School had started only a week ago, but the teachers at Rolling Hills Elementary don't believe in wasting any time. They get right to torturing their students . . . kind of like the Puritans.

Olive whizzed past me.

"I'll get it." She raced to the door and yanked it open.

A plain white envelope lay on the stoop. My name and address were written in big block letters. No postage. No return address.

My stomach flip-flopped. I recognized the handwriting. It was the same that had been on the package with the crystal radio in it. I swallowed hard. I knew who it was from: H.H.

It was just one sentence:

*The leftovers fit together.*

"Huh?" said Olive. "What leftovers?

Those prunes from Ellie's breakfast?" She shivered. "Nothing fits with those."

"Leftovers," I muttered, thinking.

I went upstairs to my bedroom, opened my desk drawer, and took out the hairnet Eleanor had left behind. Ben had left something too. Still thinking, I headed out into the garage. That was where I'd put the electrostatic machine we'd built with Ben. I'd stuck it in the corner behind the snowblower and covered it with a tarp.

I pulled away the tarp.

It didn't look like anything special, just an old ice cream maker with a bunch of random parts attached to it. But I knew that as I cranked the handle, it would generate tiny sparks of electricity.

The machine whirred and hummed. Pinpricks of blue electricity lit up the glass jars on top.

The hairnet in my hand began to wiggle as if it were alive.

"Ugh!" I cried, opening my fingers.

Freed, the hairnet twisted like a jellyfish, changing shape and size. It stretched itself over the generator. And as it did, the electrostatic machine seemed to grow in strength. The electric charge blazed bluer. The soft whirr changed to a low roar.

"What's going on?" asked Olive, coming into the garage.

"I . . . I'm not sure," I said.

But as we stood there staring at the contraption, stuff started to dawn on me. I had this strange feeling that the contraption wasn't finished. That it needed more parts. I swear I could almost see a pattern in my mind, a sense of pieces snapping into place. But what sorts of pieces? And why? What were we building?

My gut told me it had to do with the radio. And H.H.

The machine hummed, and sparks crawled over the hairnet until it glowed blue-white. Then it flickered out and whirred to silence, shutting itself down.

"Weeeeird!" drawled Olive.

"You can say that again."

"Weeeeird!"

We stared at the machine for another

minute. Then I threw the tarp back over it and headed up to the attic.

I must have looked determined, because Olive chased after me. "What are you going to do, Nolan?" she asked.

I hadn't touched the radio since hiding it in the attic after our pizza party with Mom and Mr. Selff. I hadn't wanted Olive to touch it either, so I'd put it in with Christmas stuff, buried under a ginormous knot of indoor-outdoor lights. I figured if no one played with the radio, nobody from history could turn up. But the note from H.H. had me worried. I had to see it. Make sure it was still there. Make sure it was still off.

I dug around in the cardboard box, pulled the radio out, and set it on the dusty wooden floor. When I opened the hinged lid, I relaxed a little: the thing was dark and quiet.

"The radio!" yelped Olive from my door-way. "It's the radio!"

She danced into the room. "Hey, I've got an idea. Let's call Ellie. Or . . . wait . . . let's call Ben. Or . . . no . . . I know . . . let's call them both!" She grabbed for the dial.

I grabbed at her. "No, Olive! Stop!"

*POP!*

A bright white light shot across the room. It grew white . . . whiter . . . crystal white. From within its depths came the sounds of static and faint voices.

"I'm just a hunka, hunka ... *khhhh* ... hound dog ... *khhhh* ... left the building ... *khhhh* ..."

"Here we go again!" squealed Olive.

I braced myself.

# WHAT NOLAN KNOWS

The day after Eleanor left, I headed over to the library to do some research on her stories. I didn't think she'd lied or anything. I mean, we're talking *Eleanor Roosevelt* here. But I'd done the same thing after Ben's visit—double-checked his facts—so it seemed only fair.

Here's what I learned:

I hope you didn't use Factopedia!

## STORY #1: FALA MAKES A MOVIE

Fala really was a movie star. In December 1942, directors from the Metro-Goldwyn-Mayer Studios in Hollywood arrived at the White House to make *The President's Dog.* Directors planned on filming Fala doing all kinds of dog stuff, like chasing squirrels and digging up bones—a typical day in his life.

What? No explosions or car chase? Boooring!

Fala was already famous. Since his arrival at the White House as a puppy in late 1940, Americans had been reading stories about his antics. And they were crazy for him. I mean *nuts.* Every week, he got bags of fan mail. People sent him letters, pictures of their own pets, rubber bones, and stuffed toys. Fala got so much mail Eleanor finally had to hire him his own secretary to handle it all.

Those Hollywood directors were pretty confident they'd have a hit on their hands . . . if only they could get the stubborn Scottie to cooperate. It wasn't until Eleanor suggested bribing Fala with bacon that he finally started acting. Good thing, too, because the director had brought along a stunt double just in case.

The following spring, *The President's Dog* hit theaters. Shown before the main feature, it was short—just ten minutes long—and was what studios called a morale booster. That is, it was made specifically to cheer people up and take their minds off their troubles. And boy, did people have troubles just then! A year earlier, the United States had entered World War II. Hundreds of thousands of Americans were far from their homes, fighting across Europe and the Pacific. They needed all the morale boosting they could get. Fala's movie did just that. Reporters called him a dog hero. And President Roosevelt praised him for doing his "bit for the war effort." In fact, the Scottie's film was so popular that a couple of years later, Hollywood directors made a second one—*Fala at Hyde Park.*

## STORY #2: HOT DOG PICNIC

Eleanor really *did* throw a hot dog picnic for the king and queen of England at the Roosevelt family estate in Hyde Park, New York, in 1939. King George really *did* scarf down two hot dogs. Queen Elizabeth really *did* turn all flustered and ask how to eat it. And get this: FDR really *did* tell her to "push it into your mouth and keep pushing until it's gone." Ha! He said that to a *queen*! Geez, that President Roosevelt must have been some funny guy. Too bad the queen didn't take his advice. Instead, she really *did* cut up her hot dog with a knife and fork.

But here's what Eleanor *didn't* tell us about the picnic.

Back in 1939, many Americans didn't like the British royalty. They still believed the king was an evil colonial ruler. No kidding. They were holding grudges for like . . . one hundred and fifty years!

FDR wanted to change their thinking. He knew it was only a matter of time before World War II broke out in Europe, and he wanted to be able to help England when it did. So he encouraged Eleanor to throw a simple, all-American picnic. Sure, the event looked casual and sort of tossed together, but a lot of thought went into it. Anyway, the plan worked. The picnic was a success. Not only did the royals and the Roosevelts became good friends, but the next day, the front page of the *New York Times* read, "King Tries Hot Dog, Asks for More."

This changed people's opinion of the king. Suddenly, they saw him as a regular guy who gobbled hot dogs off paper plates just like they did.

When war did erupt in Europe three months later, Americans felt bad for their new royal friends. It didn't take much for FDR to convince them to send money and supplies. Good thing, too, because without that help, England would probably have lost the war within months.

Yay for hot dogs!

## STORY #3: FLYING WITH AMELIA

In Eleanor's time, air travel was still new, and most people thought it was dangerous. They stuck to trains or cars. But not the First Lady. If she could, she always traveled by plane. She hoped her example would encourage others to fly, and prove to them that airplanes were safe.

Flying, of course, is what brought Eleanor and Amelia Earhart together. In November 1932—just days after her husband was elected president—Eleanor drove to Poughkeepsie, New York.

Po . . . whatsie?

That's where Amelia Earhart was giving a speech about her flying adventures. When she finished, Eleanor introduced herself and told Amelia about her love of airplanes. Right away, Amelia offered to teach her to fly. She even helped Eleanor get her student pilot's license. By the time they went on that night flight six months later, they were best friends.

Heading out to an airfield in Arlington, Virginia, they borrowed a small passenger plane owned by Eastern Airlines. I know that sounds sort of crazy, but I guess if you're Eleanor Roosevelt or Amelia Earhart, people will lend you anything . . . even an airplane! The women flew to Baltimore and back. Amelia was at the controls most of the time, with Eleanor in the seat beside her.

They weren't entirely alone, though. Since she didn't mention him in her story, Eleanor must have forgotten that her brother, Hall, went along. So did Amelia's husband, George Putnam. They rode in the main cabin, along with two Eastern Airlines pilots and a group of women reporters. Geez, talk about a crowd.

Later, they all went back to the White

House. And here's where history gets a little foggy. Some historians say that afterward, Eleanor drove Amelia around in her roadster, which is a 1930s kind of car. Others don't mention it at all. Was it true or not? (Finally, I asked Mrs. Bustamante. I mean, if a librarian can't help you, who can? Anyway, she handed me a book by Pam Muñoz Ryan that includes the car ride story. She says Ms. Ryan is a "trustworthy source," so I'm going with it.)

In July 1937, while trying to fly around the world, Amelia disappeared. She was never heard from again. When Eleanor heard the news, she cried. She told reporters that she was sure her friend's last words were "I have no regrets."

## STORY #4: SAD LITTLE ELEANOR

The Roosevelt family had wealth, power, and high social status. But none of it brought young Eleanor any happiness. That's because her mother, Anna, treated her coldly and called her names like "ugly duckling" and "Granny."

Her father, Elliott, made her feel safe and loved. But Elliott wasn't around much. An alcoholic, he often disappeared for weeks on end. Eventually, Anna separated from him. Eleanor—who was just five at the time—was too little to understand why. All she knew was that life was scary and confusing without him. She started keeping more and more to herself.

Thank goodness her father took her to the Newsboys' Lodge that Thanksgiving morning in 1890. Despite his personal problems, he wanted to teach his six-year-old about doing good works.

It was sort of a Roosevelt family tradition that they use their power and position to help those less fortunate. They started schools and hospitals in New York City's slums. They even built the Newsboys' Lodge for homeless boys who made their living selling newspapers on the streets. And here's the thing: The family didn't just give money to these charities. They rolled up their sleeves and got to work!

That day, Eleanor scooped potatoes and served slices of pie. By late afternoon, she was tired. She was also full of good feelings. She didn't feel unattractive and inferior. She didn't feel scared or unhappy. "The feeling that I was useful was perhaps the greatest joy I experienced," she later said about that day.

From that moment on, Eleanor devoted herself to helping others. When she grew up, she worked in slums and taught under-privileged kids. Later, she fought for civil rights and racial justice for African Americans. She championed women's rights. She was even appointed to the first American delegation to the United Nations and wrote a document called the Declaration of Human Rights. It stated that all people deserved liberty and equality, no matter their race, religion, or nationality. All this and more earned her the nickname First Lady of the World.

You go, Ellie!

P.S. Remember that Horatio guy? He's a character in a famous play called *Hamlet*. In it, Horatio's best friend, Hamlet, claims he has talked to a ghost. No way does Horatio believe him. So Hamlet says, "There are more things in heaven and earth, Horatio, than are dreamt of in your philosophy." Huh! That's the very line both Eleanor and

Mr. Selff quoted. Since it's written in Ye Olde English or something, it's kind of hard to understand. But basically it means this: the universe is full of unexplainable mysteries.

Boy, did Hamlet ever get that right!

Just in case you want to fact-check Eleanor's stories yourself, here are the books I used, also called my

## BIBLIOGRAPHY

Cooney, Barbara. *Eleanor*. New York: Puffin Books, 1999.

Fleming, Candace. *Our Eleanor: A Scrapbook Look at Eleanor Roosevelt*. New York: Atheneum Books for Young Readers, 2005.

Freedman, Russell. *Eleanor Roosevelt: A Life of Discovery*. New York: Clarion Books, 1997.

Kimmelman, Leslie. *Hot Dog! Eleanor Roosevelt Throws a Picnic*. Ann Arbor, MI: Sleeping Bear Press, 2014.

Rappaport, Doreen. *Eleanor, Quiet No More*. New York: Disney-Hyperion, 2009.

Ryan, Pam Muñoz. *Amelia and Eleanor Go for a Ride*. New York: Scholastic Press, 1999.

Suckley, Margaret L., and Alice Dalgliesh. *The True Story of Fala*. Delmar, NY: Black Dome Press, 1997.

Thompson, Gare. *Who Was Eleanor Roosevelt?* New York: Grosset & Dunlap, 2004.

The First Lady is definitely "Everywhere Eleanor" when it comes to the internet. There are gazillions of websites about her, as well as videos and photos. Here are my favorites:

### youtube.com/watch?v=qpVNY5FJCis

This is it! Snippets from Fala's star performance in *The President's Dog.* I laughed at the scenes with the scrapbook. You can totally tell by Fala's excited behavior that the pages are sprinkled with bacon. It's the same way he acted when he got a whiff of Tommy's trench coat.

### youtube.com/watch?v=oSMV5zxHaxc

A great biography put together for Eleanor's 125th birthday, this video is full of newsreel clips and photographs. Not to sound sappy or anything, but it was just so good to see Eleanor again, you know?

### youtube.com/watch?v=6HY8vxYX78s

And because it's so weird, here's a short clip of Eleanor doing a commercial for Good Luck Margarine. See what I mean about her fluttery voice? By the way, any money she made from doing commercials she gave to charity.

**CANDACE FLEMING** is the author of *Ben Franklin's in My Bathroom!*, the first funny title in this hysterical series, as well as the middle-grade novels *The Fabled Fourth Graders of Aesop Elementary* and *The Fabled Fifth Graders of Aesop Elementary*. She writes nonfiction books, too, including *The Great and Only Barnum, Amelia Lost,* and *Our Eleanor,* which is also about Eleanor Roosevelt. Once, Candace followed Eleanor's recipe for her favorite dessert: blueberry pudding. It called for blueberries, white bread, and cream. And guess what? It turned out a soggy mess. Candace lives in Illinois, but you can visit her on the Web at candacefleming.com.

**MARK FEARING** is the illustrator of *Ben Franklin's in My Bathroom!* and more than a dozen picture books, including *Chicken Story Time* by Sandy Asher and *Three Little Aliens and the Big Bad Robot* by Margaret McNamara. Growing up, Mark knew of Eleanor Roosevelt and her husband, Franklin, because his parents lived through the Great Depression. As he gets older, he is even more impressed with the issues Eleanor championed, and keeps in mind a saying often credited to her: "It takes as much energy to wish as it does to plan." Mark lives with his wife, daughter, and dog in Oregon. Visit him on the Web at markfearing.com.